SUMMER IS A SHORT SEASON

SECOND EDITION

BOOK THREE OF THE FOUR PART SERIES

SOULLESS

BY

SUMMER SELINE COYLE

ACACIA LEAF PRESS

S S E Publishing & Acacia Leaf Press. Rothesay

As buried secrets come to light, the Horncastle empire crumbles under the weight of its secrets and lies. A disadvantaged Jack embarks on a perilous journey that takes him across the U. S. A chance meeting with a familiar face from the past alters the course of his life. **SUMMER IS A SHORT SEASON** is the third book in the SOULLESS Series.

SEXUAL THEMES, VIOLENCE, STRONG LANGUAGE, EMOTIONAL TRIGGERS, LGBTQ THEMES.

"A captivating plot with many surprising twists and turns. The characters are well developed and intense relationships are formed. As in real life, there are many highs and lows in these relationships."

The Selective Reader

This novel is dedicated to my beautiful daughter, Lyla, who is a joy and an inspiration to me.

SUMMER IS A SHORT SEASON

SECOND EDITION

BOOK THREE OF THE **SOULLESS** SERIES

TABLE OF CONTENTS

Chapter 1/ A SUMMER STORM

August had been behaving like a capricious mistress, her Southern winds whipping branches off unsuspecting trees, her rains flooding basements without mercy, her thunder storms wreaking havoc with electricity. A cruel August was often followed by a kind September, and Dottie hoped that would happen this autumn.

She had spent the day with Clara, shopping downtown (Clara doing the shopping and she tagging along), eating hamburgers and watching "Tootsie" at the aging movie theater before Clara left for Toronto. At her small college, a Bachelor of Arts was a three year program, instead of four as in most universities, and Clara was now returning for her one year Bachelor of Education degree. They parted company at the corner of Aberdeen and Westmorland Streets, and Clara continued up the hill. Believing it would save time, Dottie made the decision to follow Aberdeen as far as it stretched, to turn left on Church Street and to follow it to Waterloo Row. Storm clouds were gathering overhead, and she prayed the rain would hold out until she made it home. Soon, however, she became aware of the error in her decision along the isolated, unlit patch of Aberdeen between York and Carleton Streets, with vacant lots, construction trailers, ramshackle sheds, abandoned businesses, overgrown shrubbery, and a long stretch of fields extending to the railroad tracks. Under an ominous sky, she ran swiftly in her scuffed sneakers. She realized hers were not the only set of footsteps on the pavement. She sped up as the footsteps behind her drew closer, however, the stranger had a wider stance and was able to catch up to her effortlessly. She opened her mouth to scream, but a hand closed over it. She groaned and attempted to kick him, but felt a sharp blade against her back.

"Don't make a sound." a gruff voice commanded, "Listen, Junior Detective: Stop meddling in things that don't concern you. You dig?"

"Hmm." she nodded.

"If you don't do as you're told, you'll be next."

Before she could finally breathe, his thin dark figure in denim was swiftly swallowed up by the dark landscape of the open fields. She ran, breathless and numb, back to the corner of York Street and knocked firmly on the side door of the aging grey building, where she had, during one of her long treks with Clara, observed a thin, middle-aged woman performing crossing-guard duties. The door was promptly opened and the familiar face greeted her with a smile.

"I'm sorry to trouble you, but could you please call me a cab?" she blurted out.

"What's wrong, honey? You look like you've seen a ghost." the woman motioned her to enter the dim, narrow foyer, "I'll get you some water."

"I don't want to be any trouble." she took a tentative step inside; the aroma of fried fish made her realize how hungry she was, "A man tried to attack me half a block from here and I don't want to walk home by any other route after that. I hope you don't mind calling me a cab."

"Come in. Sit down, honey." the woman called out toward the living room on her left, "Len, can you get this young lady a glass of water?...You poor thing. I'll call the police, dear, so you can give them details. They might be able to catch him."

"Thank you. You're very kind."

A grey-haired, bespectacled man joined them with a glass of water and handed it to Dottie. The woman disappeared into the living room and dialed the phone.

"Yes...I'm at the corner of York and Aberdeen, and a young lady's been assaulted on the stretch of Aberdeen between York and Carleton...Yes, just a minute...Honey, can you come in and talk to the 911 operator?"

Dottie wiped her feet on the black doormat and entered the living room with well-worn furniture covered in earth-toned crocheted afghans.

"Hello." she took the phone, "Yes, I'm the one who was assaulted...He came up behind me and covered my mouth. He held a knife to my back and threatened me...Then, he ran off toward the railroad tracks. He was thin, dressed in jeans and a denim jacket...Fairly young. Yes, the address is..." She turned to the woman.

"326 York Street."

"326 York Street." she repeated, "It's right on the corner of Aberdeen, toward Carleton. My name? Dorothy Horncastle. Okay, sure. Thank you. Bye." She handed the phone back to the woman, "I'm sorry to be so much trouble. They want me to wait here."

"No problem, honey. Have a seat. We were watching "I Love Lucy"."

"You missed it because of me."

"We've seen this episode a dozen times. Sit down."

9

"Would you like some cookies?" Len offered.

"No, thank you. Please don't miss any more of your show."

The minutes were like hours. Then, there was a knock on the door, and a clearly audible "This is the police.". Dottie sprang up and opened the door.

"Are you Dorothy Horncastle?" the middle-aged officer asked.

"Yes."

"Come in, Officer." the woman turned off the television and joined them.

"It's all right, Ma'am. I'll take down the information here." he produced his pen and notepad, "This guy came up from behind you?"

"Yes. I heard footsteps behind me, tried to outrun him, but he was too quick. He put a hand over my mouth and held a knife to my back."

"What did he say to you?"

"To stop meddling in things that didn't concern me, or I'd be next."

"Did he demand money?"

"No."

"Would you recognize his voice if you heard it again?"

"Definitely."

"We've caught a guy by the old train station. We'd like you to come to the station and see if you can recognize his voice."

"That was pretty quick." the woman piped up, "You boys are real heroes."

"Thank you, Ma'am."

"Phyllis, please."

"We're only three blocks from here, so the bozo didn't stand a chance. Now, Miss, I'll take you to the police station to see if you can recognize his voice."

"Of course." she turned to Phyllis, "Thank you so much, Phyllis, for everything."

"You're welcome, honey. You come back any time for a proper visit."

"I'd like that. Bye." she waved on her way out to the police cruiser.

The officer opened the front passenger's side door for her.

"I'm glad I don't have to sit in the back where the crooks sit." she said.

* * *

"It's #4. I have no doubt." she stated matter-of-factly after listening to seven men utter: "Don't make a sound. Listen, Junior Detective: Stop meddling in things that don't concern you. You dig? If you don't do as you're told, you'll be next."

"You have an amazing memory." a younger officer remarked, "Even under great stress, you recalled every word he spoke."

"Thank you. God was looking out for me."

"I think so, too. I'll take you home now, Miss Horncastle." he led her outside to the police cruiser and opened the door for her, "If you think of anything else you think we need to know, feel free to call."

"Thank you."

"I'm Constable Jack Callaghan."

"Wait!" she exclaimed in sudden realization.

"Did you remember something?"

"Yes! Your name just made me realize something. I don't know why it didn't register before."

"My name?"

"Yes. This has to do with my cousin Jack. Of course, it all makes sense now."

"Sounds intriguing. Can you enlighten me?"

"My cousin Jack was in a bad fire at his club last winter."

"Yes – the Willow Place fire...Your cousin was Jack Chandler. I'm sorry for your loss."

"He was declared dead, but my uncle and my other cousin believed Jack's stepmother, my aunt, did something to fake his death in order to come between him and his new bride, who, by the way, is also my cousin from the other side of the family."

"Fascinating. Go on."

"So, my uncle, my cousin, his girlfriend, my best friend and I started investigating on our own. In the spring, I came across some crucial information: A homeless man who bore an uncanny physical resemblance to my cousin Jack had gone missing just before Jack's death was announced. I brought our suspicions to some of your colleagues' attention at the time. This guy's got to be connected to that. I think we got too close to the truth and they are panicking. My uncle believes my aunt is getting help from very influential people in this cover-up. This thug's one of their flunkies – just a minor player in the whole scheme."

"You're pretty knowledgeable, Miss Horncastle. You'd make an excellent member of our team."

"Thank you. I watch a lot of police dramas." she realized they were in front of her house and the car had stopped, "How did you know where I lived?"

"Everyone knows where the Horncastles live." he smiled, "Thank you, Miss Horncastle, for coming to the station and identifying the suspect. I'll definitely look into the file about the missing man."

"Thank you for everything, Officer."

"If you think of anything else, don't hesitate to call me."

"I won't have any trouble remembering your name."

"You take care, Miss, and stay safe."

"You, too, Officer. Thank you for the ride home."

"My pleasure. Have a good night."

"You have a good night, too."

He waited in the driveway until she opened the side door with her key and waved at him.

Dottie called out "Hello" into the silent house.

Maxine, Marge's replacement, emerged from the basement in her jade paisley caftan and with her long, unruly dark curls tied back in a loose ponytail.

"Miss Dottie, you're back. Did you have a nice day?"

"A very eventful one, Maxine. I'm just glad to be home."

"You look exhausted. I'll put on some chamomile tea."

"Maxine, is Warren home?"

"No, Miss. He's closing a deal in New Maryland, but he should be back soon. If you like, I can leave a note under his door for him to see you when he gets in."

"Thank you. That would be nice, Maxine."

"I've got some freshly baked carrot muffins. Would you like some?"

"I'd love a couple. Is Peggy in, by any chance?"

"She's staying at her parents' apartment for the night. Her mom's taken ill, so she's taking care of her. Tell you what, Miss: I'll draw you a nice hot bath and bring up the tea and muffins to your room."

"That would be fantastic, Maxine."

Maxine placed a motherly arm around her and led her up to the third floor.

Dottie's room had morphed from the dreamy, ethereal sanctuary to a modern, bright spot. Gone were the cloud motif wallpaper, the white eyelet and white wicker. The sofa had been replaced with a second bed. The walls were painted a vibrant rose color; the bedspreads and curtains were a rose and mint floral; the furniture was blush oak. A rose and cream floral print rug concealed the old white shag carpeting. A compact television set was strategically placed on a shelf. Despite the fact that her parents were no longer the housekeeper and groundskeeper, Peggy had remained in the house as her roommate. She had free room and board in exchange for performing kitchen duties on the weekends as Aunt Mildred had stipulated.

The warmth of the bath water soothed her aching muscles as she placed her head on the rubber tub pillow and closed her eyes. She could not wait to see the look on Peggy's face tomorrow when she told her that a young, handsome officer with a special name had given her a ride home.

Chapter 2/ SUMMER CLOUDS

"Good morning." Roberta entered the sun-filled room, "How are you doing, honey?"

"Good morning, Roberta."

"Ribby, please. Lovely morning. Looks like your appetite's improving." she eyed the empty breakfast containers on his bedside table.

"I feel stronger."

"You scared us for a while there. You were unconscious for so long." she glanced at his chart, "Your vitals look strong."

"Yes. Cicely was here about fifteen minutes ago to take them."

"Changing of the guard." she smiled, "I'm your day nurse."

"Ribby, may I ask you something?"

"Sure, honey."

"Why am I here? I don't remember anything and no one'll tell me a single thing. My mom says I was in an accident."

"That's what I heard, too. Before you came around, you were calling out a name...Cindy. Is she someone special? Can you remember anything about her?"

"The name doesn't mean anything. I don't remember anything at all. I thought this only happened in the movies."

"It can happen. It's usually short-term and only the events just before the injury are erased from memory. The only time I have witnessed patients experiencing complete memory loss like this, was due to psychological trauma. Be patient with yourself, dear. It'll all come back when you're ready."

"I hope so."

"It'll happen in its own time. Don't try to push yourself to remember." she patted his shoulder, "There's your mother, now. Morning, Ma'am." she greeted the impeccably groomed, slender woman in the doorway.

"Good morning. How's Chad doing?"

"Very well. Physically, he's healing remarkably. Soon, he'll be able to remember his life, as well."

"I'm sure he will." the woman coldly observed the rotund, soft-featured, motherly woman, "Can you give us a little time alone, please?"

"Certainly, Mrs. Johnson." she responded in her professional manner; the stark white of her uniform appeared exaggerated against her flawless black skin.

"Chad, dear." the woman said, once certain Ribby was out of earshot, "You need to give it time. Dr. Mazot said it can take several weeks for those pills to take effect."

"Mom, why can't you tell me some things about my life?"

"According to Dr. Mazot, it can be detrimental to rush the process, to receive information before you're ready."

"How am I going to know when I'm ready? I'd like to know some basic facts like who I am, what I do for a living, where we're from."

"All I can tell you is you're Chad Johnson, an artist, and a high school art teacher, and we're from Vancouver, B.C."

"Why are we here?"

"Because Dr. Mazot is the best in North America. He's worked extensively with patients suffering from amnesia, and has a phenomenal success rate. You're in good hands, son."

"It just feels strange...Not remembering myself, not remembering you, or any aspect of my life...I find it odd that there's no one else in our lives – no other family or friends."

"It's just us, dear."

The pale young man's lethargic green eyes looked away from her, past the pale yellow room, past the morning sky outside his window.

"Dr. Mazot says you're going to be discharged soon."

"And go where, Mom?" he spoke indignantly, "Where's home? A hotel?"

"The Hyatt-Regency is very comfortable. And close by. It's very convenient since you need to continue seeing Dr. Mazot on an outpatient basis for several months."

"I don't think he's doing any good, Mom. Neither are his drugs. They just make me tired."

"He knows what he's doing. You're not in a position to determine the effectiveness of your therapy."

"I'm sick and tired of being in limbo. I need to move on and start building a new life if my old life is lost to me."

"Of course I want that, too, dear. You need to start over and build a new life. Just wait till Dr. Mazot gives the green light."

"I feel empty, Mom. Like a hollow shell. I want to be alive. I want to feel things again."

"Be patient, Chad, dear."

He crossed the room to the window and fixed his gaze on the clouds. Clouds...A fleeting image of a white, frothy room with cloud wallpaper flashed before his eyes...a young girl with a small frame, a dark ponytail, and laughing eyes...A wave of tenderness swept over him...She was someone he cared for deeply...someone he ached to protect from harm...Not a love interest...but family...A daughter? A sister? He shut his eyes.

"Don't get yourself all worked up, dear." his mother said.

Why had his mother insisted they had no other family? What was she concealing from him? Was there a scandalous family secret she believed he would be unable to deal with? He needed to be alone. He needed her to leave. In carefree oblivion, she rattled on behind him, her voice fading into the humming of an insect as he attempted to recapture that fleeting image...There was someone out there who was family, someone he loved, and who loved him back, and he needed to find her.

* * *

Mildred stood in the doorway, a plump sausage stuffed into a peach floral casing. Tony brushed past her and down the hallway.

"She's had plenty of time to grieve." she said, "You can take off the kid gloves now, son."

"Enough, Mom. I'm late for work."

"What does she know about running a business? The place could go under in a month. Buy her out."

"I want to respect Jack's wishes. He would never want Sydney to be treated that way. She owns fifty percent of "Jack's Place". Whether or not you like it, you have to accept it."

"What was that boy thinking? You should be the sole owner, now that he's gone. If he were alive, he would've divorced her by now, anyway."

"That's enough, Mom." Tony descended the stairs swiftly, "I don't want to hear any more about it."

"That woman destroyed our family." the sausage followed him, "Warren lost his job; Jack lost his life; you and Jack lost your businesses; Audrey had a nervous breakdown and disappeared."

"Have some respect, Mom. She's been through hell. She loved Jack very deeply."

"She didn't waste any time getting her hands on the business."

"Jack wanted her to be a business partner because he knew she wasn't like the others. She loved him for himself. She didn't want any part of the family fortune."

"She's not even living here anymore."

"She's in constant contact. Sydney's very dedicated. This is very important for her. It's a part of Jack she can hold on to. This discussion is over, Mom. I am not having any more conversations with you about Sydney. Jack was very fortunate to have found her. She made him very happy."

As though swept away by a gust of wind, he was gone, leaving Mildred on the landing, shaking her head in disbelief.

Chapter 3/ SUMMER'S END

The white lamb's tail hydrangeas were turning pale pink, signalling the end of warm days. They walked up the flagstone path to the veranda with their hands linked.

"I'll call you tomorrow." he kissed her cheek.

"Why don't you come for dinner tomorrow night?" she said.

"Me, have dinner with your folks?" he laughed.

"Then, why don't we arrange for you to have dinner when my parents, Uncle Willy and Aunt Mildred are out of town?"

"Who's going to be around to protect you from no-good bums like me when they're away?"

"Tony and Warren. They're quite harmless."

"I've never had dinner at an upper class house before."

"Don't worry. Tony and Warren don't put on airs. They're the rebels of the clan."

"Okay, then. Just for you, Miss Dorothy." he touched the tip of her nose, "Have a good night."

"Be careful out there tonight. I worry about you when you're at work, Jack."

"No need. I'll be perfectly safe, daydreaming about you."

"You big stud." she punched his arm jovially, "My big, strong protector." she kissed his cheek.

"What do you want to do tomorrow?"

"Doesn't matter. We'll figure something out. We always do."

"I'll call you when I wake up tomorrow." he started back to his car, "Sweet dreams."

"Bye." she blew him a kiss and watched him drive down the street until distance shrunk his car to the size of an insect.

When she opened the front door with her key, she heard loud voices from Uncle Willy's den down the hall.

"Just remember: I have enough dirt on you to get you disbarred and sent away for the rest of your miserable life, you mother fucker!"

This was Warren's voice, followed by the slamming of a door. Warren's heavy footsteps started up the stairs. Dottie cowered in the corner until she heard his bedroom door close upstairs. She tiptoed into the kitchen, where she found Peggy and Maxine sitting at the table, drinking peppermint tea and munching on minibites served on a blue stoneware plate.

"Hi, Dots." Peggy beamed.

"Miss Dottie, I'll pour you some tea." Maxine rose.

"Hi, guys. Thanks, Max. It smells delicious."

"How's Jack?" Peggy winked.

"He's good. He agreed to come to dinner when Mom and Dad, Uncle Willy and Aunt Mildred are away." she sat beside her.

Maxine poured tea from the white ceramic teapot into a sky blue mug and returned to the table.

"Yummy. Somebody's been to Minnie's." Dottie stuffed a strawberry-filled bite-sized doughnut hole pastry into her mouth.

"Danny and I were at Minnie's before he brought me home. We bought a box of minibites for you guys." Peggy said, "How serious is it with you and Jack?"

"I know what you mean and the answer is no." Dottie said.

"Same here. I guess we'll always be 'good girls'."

"Nothing wrong with that." Maxine said.

"I guess Clara's in love." Dottie picked up another miniature treat and looked at it pensively.

"Again?" Peggy laughed.

"This time, it's real, I guess. They're talking about moving in together."

"How long have they known each other? Two weeks?"

"Maybe it's Kismet." Maxine said.

"I don't feel ready for that type of commitment." Dottie mused, "Doing someone's laundry, cooking his meals, keeping an apartment reasonably clean, trying to look presentable at all times...It would feel like life on another planet. It's one thing to care about someone and enjoy his company, but to live with him day in and day out, to be ready to put out when he's in the mood...That's a whole other ball game. I couldn't give up these girl talk sessions in the kitchen with my two buds. I wouldn't feel whole. This is warm, safe, and cozy. I would be lost without you guys."

"Likewise." Peggy squeezed her hand.

"Yes, Miss. These nightly rituals are priceless for me." Maxine said, "Glenn and I – we've been married so long, we each have our own hobbies and friends, but we rely on each other for moral support and companionship."

"You're so lucky you met the right man, Max." Dottie said, "The thought of ending up with the wrong man scares me. I don't want to get hurt. The deeper you're in, the more it hurts."

"You have to protect your heart." Maxine patted her back.

"Speaking of broken hearts, have you spoken with Sydney recently, Dots?" Peggy asked.

"She called on Sunday. She's not doing well at all."

"Is she still living in her uncle's coach house and working at his antique shop?"

"Yes. She's become good friends with the man who rents the other half of the coach house – a gay man in his fifties. I'm glad she has a friend to talk to."

"I wish I could've met her." Maxine said, "She sounds like such an intriguing lady."

"She'll be here for the re-opening of Willow Place once it's completed. I miss her terribly." Dottie said, "But I understand that she needs a complete break from everything, so she can start healing."

Healing. She wondered if anyone had ever mastered that elusive skill, and if they would be willing to illuminate mere mortals like herself, who were absolutely inept at it.

* * *

"Willy's been cheating on me!" The overstuffed sausage was buzzing around in circles like a thwarted hornet in search of a sympathetic ear, waving a small envelope in her hand.

"What's wrong, Millie?" Annette descended the stairs in her red chenille robe.

"Willy's been cheating on me!" she held the envelope in her face.

"What? How do you know?"

"Just look!" she pressed the envelope into her hand.

"What is this?" Annette fumbled with it.

"Read what it says."

"Alice Johnson – no return address. It's typed and addressed to Willy's office. I don't understand."

"Read what's inside."

Annette removed a single typed sheet of paper and read it out loud:

"'Dear Willard...We're doing well. All problems have been taken care of for the time being. I'll keep you posted. H.M. has been a great help. Thank you for everything you've done for us. Love, Alice.'...I don't understand, Millie...Where did you get this?"

"From his den. After he left for work, I went in there to borrow one of his Schaeffer pens to write a birthday card to my friend Elsie in Maine. I noticed this on his desk."

"If he were having a secret dalliance, he wouldn't leave it lying around." Annette said.

"It might have been an oversight. It might have fallen out of a file he was putting in his briefcase."

"It's an odd letter. There's nothing flowery or romantic in it. It sounds like a colleague or an employee he might have helped with a problem. She says 'we'. She might be referring to a husband."

"Or she could be referring to a love child the two of them have. Maybe she doesn't sound romantic because they've been carrying on a clandestine relationship for decades and they're like an old married couple."

"Millie, you've been reading too many romance novels. It's probably a business associate he helped. There might have been a sick husband, a financial crisis, something perfectly innocent."

"Willard's not that charitable."

"Maybe this person helped him cover up something that wasn't up to snuff, and he was returning the favor."

"That's more plausible."

"Come on. Don't fret about stuff like this. We could speculate about this forever. The possibilities are endless with such a vague letter. Why don't you ask him about it?"

"No. He'd only lie."

"Do you want me to mention it to Donald?"

"Would you, dear? Can you ask him to be discreet?"

"Of course. He might be able to find out more about this Alice Johnson and where she actually lives. Willard's most likely keeping their correspondence and anything related to her at the office."

"Thank you, Annette, dear. I'd like to know where she lives. Even the stamp was torn off the envelope, so there's no clue."

"Don't worry, Millie. It'll all turn out to be nothing but a tempest in a teapot. You'll see." she placed an arm around her and led her toward the solarium at the back of the house, "Maxine!" she called out, "Can you get us some coffee and bring it out to the solarium?"

"Yes, Ma'am." Maxine replied.

"Come on, dear. Let's go sit in the sun, read the morning paper, enjoy some coffee and gossip about the neighbors."

Chapter 4/ THE LAST SUMMER ROSE

She cast one final glance at herself in the bathroom mirror before answering her door. He stood in the hallway with an impish grin, holding a bouquet of apricot roses.

"They're beautiful." she motioned him to enter her apartment.

"Not as beautiful as you." he said.

"I'll bet you say that to all the girls." she stuck her tongue out at him, "Have a seat. I'll put these in water."

He glanced uncomfortably around the white-carpeted living room with wicker chairs, arched wicker shelves and luxuriously tall tropical house plants. He sat at the edge of the green and coral tropical print sofa. She returned from the kitchen with a crystal vase displaying the roses and placed it on the amber glass coffee table.

"Would you like a soda before we leave?" she asked.

"No thanks. I thought we'd get an early start to take advantage of the nice weather."

"I agree. We don't know how many more warm days we have left. I'll get my sweater and handbag." she disappeared down the corridor and re-emerged with a lightweight white cardigan slung across her back and tied around her neck, and a small tan beaded shoulder bag, "The days are getting shorter at an alarming pace."

"I don't remember beautiful autumn days like these."

"Are you kidding me?" she locked her apartment door, "I would've thought you had this warm weather all year around in Vancouver. Isn't it just like California?"

"I honestly don't know, Cicely." he frowned, "I don't have any memories of living in Vancouver at all."

"I'm sorry." she touched his elbow in reassurance as they descended the front stairs of her brownstone.

"I do have one memory about Vancouver...but it doesn't make any sense."

"Why doesn't it make sense, Chad?"

"Because I remember being in a hotel – and something about the name of the hotel was significant to me...But I can't remember the name. Why would I be staying at a hotel if I lived in Vancouver?"

"Very intriguing, indeed."

"I remember writing a postcard to someone because something about the hotel was significant for them, as well."

"You're a real man of mystery, Chad Johnson. I'd love to see your artwork sometime. Your mother says you made your living as an artist. Portraits and landscapes."

"I've tried to paint, but I can't remember how to do that, either. Everything I produce looks like a little kid did it."

"Ribby says, even when we lose our memory, the skills we had before remain with us. It's got to be locked in there, somewhere. The right trigger will release it. You need to be patient with yourself, Chad."

"Mom keeps telling me Dr. Mazot is going to help me unlock my memories, but I'm not finding him very helpful at all."

"Ribby's been concerned about all the high doses of drugs he's been prescribing you. She says it's a powerful cocktail of psychogenic drugs that can have devastating consequences. You've got Elavil, your antidepressant, Stelazine, your antipsychotic, and Serax, your sedative, all in very high doses. Even in cases of the most severe clinical depression, the doses aren't customarily that high. She thinks there's something fishy."

"No wonder I feel so dopey all the time."

"You leave it with us. Ribby and I are going to get to the bottom of this. Dr. Mazot's been investigated a number of times for unethical behavior, but nothing's been able to stick. Chad, there's something else...I don't know how to tell you this..."

"Let it all hang out, Cece."

"I hope you won't be offended."

"Nothing you say could offend me."

"Ribby witnessed an interaction between your mother and an older gentleman outside Dr. Mazot's office last week."

"Like a boyfriend?"

"Not sure. Ribby said he was a well-dressed, distinguished looking older gentleman. They hugged and spoke in hushed tones. Then, they went into Mazot's office together."

"How odd. Why would she go to see Dr. Mazot with some strange man? I haven't met any men Mom is acquainted with here. I don't know when she would have the time to meet anyone."

"Ribby said, though she couldn't make out most of what they were whispering, she distinctly heard her say:

'That gold-digging lounge singer...'. Do you have any idea who she was referring to?"

"No idea. I can't imagine her going out at night to any nightclubs to hear singers."

"That's just it. Nothing makes sense. I hope I'm not overstepping my boundaries, but, Chad, I must implore you to be careful about what you share with your mother. I think she has a lot at stake in keeping you locked in your amnesiac state. I'd like to know what she's keeping from you. Chad, please don't let her know about us seeing each other, either. I don't think she'd approve."

"You're right. She's probably racist."

"It's not only because I'm black. My being a nurse at the hospital would make her suspicious and uncomfortable."

"You're absolutely right, Cece."

"Now that we're at the park, let's just enjoy the day."

He smiled and took her hand in his. Gazing at her in the sun, he noticed just how beautiful she was and wondered why he had not noticed it before. In her sunny yellow dress, she shimmered like the last yellow rose of the season hanging onto the final days of summer before becoming a casualty of frost. Her closely-cropped hair accentuated her exquisite features. With her long lashes and enormous eyes, she had the appearance of a gazelle.

Despite the warm weather, the oak tree providing shade for their bench was shedding its brown leaves, sending them fluttering. The canopy of sturdy, wise trees in the park clad in gold and vermillion were laying a carpet for the frolicking children. At a nearby bench, a grey-haired couple watched the children, smiling wistfully. A young couple walked by their bench. The young man was carrying a ghetto blaster, tuned to an oldies station. The mid-1960's popular song by "The Toys", "A Lover's Concerto" began to play and he was suddenly filled with an inexplicable sense of yearning and loss. He closed his eyes to fight back the tears that threatened to escape.

Those dewy brown eyes and that shy smile dancing on the periphery of his consciousness returned.

"I love you,..." she whispered, "I love you,..."

She spoke a name after "I love you"...Was it Chad? It slipped ever so softly off her lips...It was one syllable. If it was not Chad, then, it had to be a similar sounding name with the same "a" sound. A voice at the back of his mind was adamant it was not Chad. Had he lived under a different identity, perhaps in a place other than Vancouver?

"Where did you just go?" Cicely nudged him playfully.

"Huh?"

"You just zoned out."

"It's that song...the one that just got over."

"'A Lover's Concerto'? I love that one."

"I had a flashback...a woman's face...We were listening to the song – only, it was a different rendition...a slower instrumental one...She was saying 'I love you', and a name...But it wasn't Chad."

"You're a very intriguing man, Chad Johnson."

"I keep seeing that face in my dreams."

"You were calling out a woman's name when you were first regaining consciousness...before Mazot got his filthy hands on you. I remember Tash and Jess telling me about it. What was it?...Cindy? I think that's what they said. Does that name mean anything to you?"

"...Cindy...Not really. I don't think I know anyone by that name."

"It's good to have you back..." a new memory flashed before him.

"Good to be back. I hope you're still enjoying yourself here."

"Very much. I'm grateful to you for giving me this opportunity ..." she spoke that name again. A name that was not Chad.

Where was he back to, and where had he been? And the memory faded.

"I need to establish some financial independence." he said suddenly, "I need to distance myself from Mom."

"I don't think she has your best interest at heart. She wants to keep you doped up, getting ECT, and hypnosis from that quack."

"I'll start looking for a job. Maybe some janitorial work."

Smiling fondly, Cicely took both his hands and studied them.

"Your hands look and feel like they haven't done any work. Certainly not any manual labor. Not even art. I think you had a different occupation. Something that provided you with a comfortable lifestyle. Your hands are soft as silk."

"Maybe I can sell shoes or something."

"That would be a good start. We need to get you away from that drug pusher Mazot, somehow. I have an idea: We can have an adventure. A road trip across Canada."

"What about your job?"

"I'll go on stress leave. Ribby's retiring at the end of next month. The three of us can have a ball trying to piece together the pieces of your real identity."

"Are you sure about this? How are we going to afford it, unless I work and save some money?"

"It's okay. Ribby and I can cover the expenses."

"No, I can't accept money from you. I'll get some work right away and save up for a few months first. Cece, I wouldn't even know where to start looking for the answers to my past."

"First, we'll get you weaned off those drugs. I think you'll find, not only will you be able to think more clearly, but also will be able to remember some things."

"How are we going to do that? My mother monitors every dose I take. She even checks my mouth to be sure I'm not hiding any pills under my tongue or in my cheeks."

"What an overbearing woman." she shook her head in exasperation, "Unfortunately, you can't go cold turkey with those meds. You need to be weaned off them gradually and monitored closely. Otherwise, with those high doses, you'd have severe withdrawal symptoms."

"It can't be any worse than the way it is now."

"I think I have it figured out: First, I'll take some vacation leave. We can go to my friend's family cottage in Rhode Island. We'll get you started on the weaning process. By the time my vacation time runs out, Ribby will be retired and she can stay with you until you are weaned. Then, I'll take stress leave and we can embark on our journey."

"You're a remarkable woman, Cece, to do this for someone you've only met recently."

"You're a good guy, Chad. I hate seeing you victimized by Mazot and your mother. You deserve to be happy. You deserve to know who you are, where you belong, who your loved ones are...I noticed an indentation on the ring finger of your left hand. This woman you're remembering...I think you're married to her. And, I think your mother wanted to split you up, so she devised this crazy scheme."

"I had no idea she was capable of such evil."

"We need to find out who this woman is and where she is, so we can reunite the two of you."

"If that option is still on the table...If she hasn't moved on..."

"We'll cross that bridge when we get to it. At least, you'll know who you are and you'll get your life back."

"What about...us?"

"We're two ships that pass in the night, Chad. We're enjoying each other's company for the time being, living one day at a time. No one knows what tomorrow has in store."

"But our paths crossed for a reason."

"Yes. To get you away from your scheming mother and back to your wife."

"I can't believe you'd do this for me, Cece. Thank you."

"Don't thank me yet. I don't know if we're going to be successful." she patted his knee, "Come on. I'm famished. Let's go to Angelo's for that Italian meal."

Chapter 5/ SOLACE

She still dreamt about him every night and awakened to the familiar emptiness that engulfed her. Drowning in the cold embrace of dawn, she went through the motions of being alive: She awoke to her alarm, showered, dressed, walked to the subway station, bought a sesame bagel, which she ate on the way and arrived at work with a coffee from the coffee shop down the street. Bookkeeping at the antique shop was an undemanding job, and, for that, she was grateful. She bought her lunch at the delicatessen two doors away, and consumed it at the back of the store. After work, she took the subway home. She changed into her old jeans and one of her bargain bin tops. While playing one of her jazz albums on the phonograph, she heated up a frozen T.V. dinner in her oven. Navigating her way through this dark tunnel without end, she stuffed her pain, tears and screams inside. Her evenings were spent reading and catching up on correspondence with her parents, Brett, Daisy (via her daughter), Dottie and Marin. None of them seemed to know what to say to her. They tiptoed around her wounds, never mentioning his name.

She did not know which was worse: Believing he really was dead, or entertaining the possibility of his being alive somewhere out there and not contacting her – for reasons she did not wish to explore.

Her parents still had no contact with the Horncastles, except Dottie. Brett was working at the record shop now. She missed Marin, who was attending nursing school. Dottie was in her final year of university, and dating a police officer named Jack Callaghan. Daisy was getting more frail, but her daughter was now living at the house to care for her. Life in

Beavertown went on as always, yet, somehow, it seemed to her as though her life in that town had never existed; it had all been a dream. Perhaps Jack, too, had been a dream. She glanced down at her left hand; her engagement and wedding rings were intact. In her heart of hearts, she needed to believe that he would, someday, return to her. She needed to believe it for the sake of her sanity. She needed to believe it in order to continue the drudgery of remaining alive against her will.

The one bright light in her existence was Eli: Eli with the laughing eyes, infectious smile, irrepressible sense of humor, and a heart so big, overflowing with so much love, no darkness could invade a room in his presence. He had appointed himself her protector and ally from the moment they had met. He lived in the other apartment in Uncle Ira and Aunt Ethel's coach house.

She smiled to herself remembering the day she had arrived.

"Hello. I'm pleased to finally meet my new neighbor. I've heard so much about you I feel I know you already." Eli emerged from his apartment, upon hearing footsteps on the stairs.

"This is Eli Rosen, your next door neighbor and master comedian." Uncle Ira introduced them, unlocking her door and handing her a set of keys on a plain metal keyring, "These two are for your apartment. The third one is for the main door downstairs."

"Thank you, Uncle Ira."

Jacob entered the apartment ahead of them and deposited her two suitcases and carry-on luggage.

"You travel light, Cousin."

"Thank you for bringing them up, Jacob."

"My pleasure, Sydney."

"Please give my best to Mimi."

"I will. Take care." he descended the stairs swiftly.

"I'll leave you two to get acquainted, then." Uncle Ira patted her on the shoulder, "Take it easy, dear. Eli'll take good care of you."

"I'll certainly try." he extended his hand, "Nice to meet you."

"Nice to meet you, too." she shook his hand.

"You must be tired and hungry. I can make dinner for us or order take-out, if you like."

"Please don't go to any trouble on my account."

"No trouble. I enjoy cooking. But I can order out if you like."

"You're very kind."

"Why don't we have some coffee and biscuits first?"

"Sounds good to me, Mr. Rosen."

"Eli, please."

"I'm Sydney."

"I know." he winked, "Don't worry; I've only heard good things."

And, Eli had been her beacon, her lifeline since that day. His smile greeted her at the top of the stairs when she returned from work. His furrowed brow greeted her on the days she missed her train and took the later one. There was someone who worried about her when she was late. She worried about him too. She softly knocked on his door to check on him when she did not hear his classical music playing. They ran errands for one another when one of them was ill, and nursed each other back to health. Their shared wall made her feel secure and protected. Sleep came more easily. She considered herself blessed.

There was a knock at her door. She could not help smiling when she found him on the other side with a bag containing Chinese take-out containers.

"Hello, Lady Sydney. I thought you might want a break from those T.V. dinners."

"Thank you, Eli."

"You know you should start accepting my invitations for dinner more often. I always cook enough for two. You don't have to be so shy."

"I don't want to impose."

"Impose! Pshaw!" he shook his head, "Or are you sick of my company?"

"You know that's not true, Eli."

"Then, you're going to let me feed you. Look at you – wasting away from hunger. No meat on your bones."

"Only if you let me reciprocate. My cooking's nothing to write home about, but I'd like to cook for you, too."

"You've got a deal."

"Eli, you're my angel. I don't know how to thank you."

"Not too many people would call a middle-aged Jewish gay man an angel."

"Don't you know middle-aged Jewish gay men make the best angels?"

"I think gorgeous young Jewish ladies make better angels. Especially ones with a unique and beautiful name like Sydney."

She kissed his cheek. He pulled her into an embrace.

"You're going to be all right, my dear Sydney." he kissed her cheek and forehead, "It's all going to work out. I really believe that."

"Thank you."

"Jack is going to come back to you. Wherever he is, he's unable to reach out to you. I just think there's a lot going on we don't know about yet. Your former adversary is doing a good job trying to expose the people behind it and locate Jack."

"You're absolutely right."

"Come on. Let's dig in. I'm famished." he removed the fast food containers from the bag and placed them on both of their placemats.

"I can't wait to dig in. Chinese is my favorite."

"Mine, too. I bought two of everything: Fried noodles, lemon chicken, beef and broccoli, and mushroom fried rice." he held her chair for her.

She placed a hand over his. On the window sill was Eli's housewarming gift to her, the tiny umbrella tree plant, secure in the knowledge that it would always be cared for and sheltered from the world outside.

Chapter 6/ SUMMER RENTAL

It was the summer neither one of them had spoken about since. It was the summer her life had changed forever. She and Warren guarded the secret with their lives and promised to take it to their graves.

She could not remember a family vacation to any destination that included all of them, in all those years since – particularly to the rented beach house in that idyllic resort in Maine. Not since the summer of 1972.

That was the summer all of them wanted to forget, the holiday no one mentioned, the summer that had altered all of their lives in ways no one could have predicted. That was also the summer she and Warren had forged that powerful bond between the two of them – the bond she had believed to be indestructible.

The summer of '72: The final, forgotten summer spent away from Beavertown...The waves nipping at her feet on the chocolate gelato shore, she was bending down to collect the pink-tinged clam shells transported by the tide. The pockets of her faded blue terrycloth beach cover were weighed down like a bulldog's jowls. On the dirt path she took home, tall weeds and wild iris tickled the backs of her calves. She came up around the back of the house, tempted by the tantalizing aroma of steaks on the charcoal fire on the back porch. The beach house was an ancient rental place with weathered white clapboard siding, broken shutters and rattling windows. Dottie imagined a gone-by era when this must have been a gracious beachfront home for a Victorian family with a healthy-sized brood, who must have played in its dark, damp rooms in their ruffled pinafores.

"Get washed up before supper!" her mother, sipping iced tea on a metal lounge chair in her green shorts, called out to her, "And get those shells out of your pockets, young lady! I don't want another incident with the washing machine like the last time!"

Her father waved his spatula in greeting and returned to the task at hand. Dottie ran into the kitchen through the rickety screen door. Aunt Mildred was tending to a pot boiling on the stove.

"You have to mash the potatoes." she reminded Dottie.

"Okey-dokey." she skipped off to the slate hallway, inhaling the stench of decaying wood and decomposing carcasses of unknown creatures under the house. Upstairs, she burst into the white bathroom. Fat, shiny beetles scurried about and hid from their intruder. She changed into her blue T-shirt and denim overalls hanging on a hook behind the door. The clear vinyl fish-print curtain circling the footed tub concealed menacing mold spores on the tile-textured wood wall behind it. The ever-expanding rust stain in the tub was a beast to be reckoned with. The nerve center of the house was the spacious living room, furnished with a claret brocade sofa and chair set in the boxy style so prevalent in the 1950's, a Colonial sofa in dark brick, cobalt, brown and olive green with a Western landscape of some sort, tacky plywood coffee and side tables in a Colonial style, and even tackier trilight lamps from the same period. The battered hardwood floors, blackened with scuff marks were covered in oilcloth in a pink dogwood print against a green background and a border of dogwood blossoms. Dottie suspected the owner had not spent a dime on renovations since the 1950's – and was now living in a clean new bungalow in the suburbs – and making a tidy profit from renting this dump to Canadian tourists. The Maloneys rented it every July and her family every August. In the evenings, her family gathered in the living room to engage in mundane discussions about politics and watch equally boring debates and newscasts on the tiny black and white television set mounted on the metal stand. She tuned them out by transfixing her gaze on the stained wallpaper: A sepia print of a country road reminiscent of the one where Andy Griffith walked with his son, Opie, on the introduction of the "Andy Griffith Show".

Jack was married to Kate then. Tony was smitten with Brett and devastated by their break-up. Kate sulked throughout the entire time she was there, complained about the lack of modern conveniences, and refused to lift a finger to help.

"Hey, kid! Take my plate to the sink!" she ordered Dottie every day, "And, get me another beer!"

At thirteen, the youngest by far, Dottie was the designated one for carrying out the chores no one else wanted to do.

"Dottie, grab a mop and clean the kitchen floor!" her mother frequently barked out orders at her.

"Make sure you get all the dead bugs in the corner!" Kate never neglected to chime in, "And that garbage is stinking up the whole house!" she added with glee.

Jack helped her with the unpleasant chores, despite protests from her mother – some spiel about teaching her responsibility. Kate wore tiny, poured-on dresses that concealed very little and tied her long red hair into two ponytails. She painted her toenails scarlet red, with clumps of toilet paper between her toes to separate them. Dottie, too, bought herself a bottle of nail polish from the General Store: Caroline brand "Petal Pink". She attempted to apply it the same way, however, spilled more of it on the bathroom floor and was sent to bed without supper. Jack smuggled half of his own meal up to her room.

Most suppers consisted of simple salads or vegetable dishes made with the fresh produce from the farmers' roadside stands: Corn on the cob, green beans, tomatoes, lettuce, zucchini, radishes and cucumbers. There were steaks or pre-formed hamburgers cooked on the old charcoal grill. For dessert, there were always fresh berries smothered in whipped cream.

The cooking duties were shared by Dottie, Jack, Tony, Aunt Audrey and Aunt Mildred. Her parents, Uncle Willy, Warren and Kate sunbathed, lounged around, and guzzled scotch all through the day and into the night.

In the evenings, she took strolls with Jack along the main street, where old men congregated on their front steps, chewing on toothpicks and gawking at the strangers invading their community. Jack bought her ice cream bars from the old General Store: Sidewalk bars, Very Cherry bars, Nutty Buddy bars, Drumstick bars. On chilly, overcast days, he bought her penny candy: Green Leaves, Shoestring Licorice, Swedish Berries, and Blue Whales. Then, her mother claimed all her teeth would fall out from the sugar she was consuming – not to mention what would happen to her already flawed complexion. Jack began buying her little trinkets, instead: Shiny red plastic earrings, plastic bangles, hair bands, barrettes and tin rings with colored glass stones, tiny plastic bubble-blowers and molded plastic dolls and animals.

Despondent Tony spent most of his time listening to Tony Bennett's record on the portable Hi-Fi, placing the needle back on "Stranger In Paradise" over and over, staring into space with wounded puppy-dog eyes. Dottie served him tall, ice-cold glasses of lemonade and fed him turkey sandwiches for lunch. He looked up at her with his lethargic Cocker Spaniel eyes.

Jack built sandcastles with her and listened to the murder mysteries she created in her own mind. Only several yards away from them, in her acid orange bikini with the lime green daisies, Kate flirted with Warren, who was listening to his transistor radio and smirking deliciously. Deafened by the sound of the crashing waves, Dottie and Jack were unable to hear what was being spoken between the two, however, Jack's furrowed brow told Dottie all she needed to know.

It was during that summer that, she learned the intricacies of relationships between men and women. It was also during that summer she had her first taste of alcohol.

According to her mother, it was unhealthy for her to be on her own or exclusively in the company of her adult cousins. She nagged her constantly to interact with other youngsters. Dottie's survival instinct was strong enough to mistrust anyone under twenty-five – with the exception of Peggy.

On most evenings, Warren slipped out to the local watering hole and did not return home until the next morning. This was hardly unusual for him, however, the entire family living in such close quarters seemed to cast a spotlight on all of their flaws and idiosyncrasies. At night, Tony called out Brett's name in his sleep. The room Dottie shared with Aunt Audrey was sandwiched between the one Tony and Warren shared (which, Tony had to himself most nights), and Jack and Kate's room, all facing the front. Her parents' room and Uncle Willy and Aunt Mildred's were the two largest ones facing the back with a view of the beach. The window of the bathroom faced the vacant lot next door. The house on that lot had burnt down long before Dottie was old enough to remember. She could hear Jack and Kate arguing at nights, often into the early hours of the morning.

"Not a chance! Not with your old battle-axe of a mother and your snotty-nosed cousin in the next room!"

"Kate, you never want to anymore."

"Is it any wonder? Use your imagination. How do you expect me to feel in the mood when you bring me to this creepy old place with the rest of your family in tow? We're cramped like sardines. There's no room to breathe, no privacy. You can hear everything through these walls. This quaint little village and rustic lifestyle might be all right for a bunch of old fogies like your relatives, but I don't want to be a fossil like the rest of you!"

"Kate, I'll make it up to you when we get back. I promise, sweetheart...Come on, give us a kiss."

"Stop grovelling, Jack. You know how much it turns me off."

"I'll make it up to you, sweetie."

"I've heard that one before, Mr. Hot Shot."

Aunt Audrey feigned sleep during these sessions, however, Dottie knew better. She could see her nose twitching.

That summer, Dottie developed her first crush on someone who was not a celebrity: Greg, the tall, tanned lifeguard at the beach wormed his way into the mystery novels in her mind, solving cases and winning the hearts of damsels in distress. She sought excuse after excuse to cross paths with him. She followed him around shamelessly.

47

"Hi, kid. How's it going?" he patted her on the head when their paths crossed, waiting in line at the canteen.

"Who is that gawky little kid who keeps following you around like a lost puppy?" a tanned svelte blonde in red shorts intercepted him on his way out one day.

"Just some tourist from up North."

"She has a hopeless crush on you! She's pathetic!" the blonde snickered and kissed him.

"No, Debbie's okay." he shrugged, "Got any smokes on you, Terri? I don't get paid till tomorrow."

Humiliated, Dottie sought sanctuary on the other side of the rocks. She reproached herself for not even having the guts to carry out the perfect plan to win his heart. Other girls would have thrown themselves into the ocean in order to be rescued by Greg. But there was a limit to how low Dottie would sink to win anyone's heart. She was proud of her swimming skills and not about to act any dumber than she already was, just to impress boys.

Warren found her there just as the storm clouds were gathering overhead.

"Come on, Shortstuff. Time to go home for supper."

"I don't want to go home." she pouted.

"There's plenty of other fish in the sea."

"How did you...?"

"You've got to get up pretty early if you want to keep anything from old Warren."

"Then, you know why I don't want to go home."

"I'll have to carry you like a sack of potatoes, then." he lifted her over one shoulder and headed home, with Dottie kicking and screaming.

As the others slept that night, with the exception of Warren, who was on his routine nocturnal prowl, Dottie tiptoed down to the living room. The rain was beating down on the flimsy tin roof and the porch overhang like a jungle drum. Dogs howled far away. The liquor cabinet was not locked. Without switching on a light, she reached for the nearest bottle and took a swig. The taste was repugnant, like cough syrup, yet warm and strangely reassuring. She did not know what it was and she did not care, as long as it gave her enough of a buzz to forget about Greg. It was not long before any lingering thoughts of him swiftly vanished. Her eyes, accustomed by now to the dark, were able to discern the words "Original Scots Whisky" beneath a drawing of a schooner ship. The slender green bottle felt warm cradled against her chest. Then, the realization struck: She had to gargle with Lavoris, so Aunt Audrey would not smell alcohol on her breath. She hummed "The Lady Is A Tramp" as she skipped up the stairs. She gargled for twenty minutes until she was convinced no trace of the smell lingered on her breath. Aunt Audrey did not even stir when she returned to the room. Dottie slept more soundly that night than she remembered.

No one questioned the absence of half a bottle of scotch. Each assumed one of the others was responsible. Dottie returned to the beach the following day and gave Greg the cold shoulder. She was proud of the way she had been able to hold her liquor. Though her gaze did not stray from "Death On The Nile", in the corner of her eye, she could see the muscular specimen rubbing sun tan lotion on Kate's back. She heard soft laughter, but was unable to make out the words spoken. Jack had gone into town with Aunt

Audrey to buy food supplies. Dottie kept reading, feigning indifference and ignorance.

During meal preparations that evening, Aunt Mildred glanced up suddenly from the salad she was tossing.

"Where's Anthony?"

"He must be up in his room, Millie, dear." Aunt Audrey said.

"Listening to Tony Bennett again, no doubt." Uncle Willy scoffed, "That son of mine is a hopeless layabout."

"All he does is mope around." Aunt Mildred said.

"Be patient, Millie. He's a sensitive lad." Aunt Audrey tasted her pasta sauce.

Then, there was a persistent knock at the front door. Dottie's dad opened it.

"Don, you'd better come down to the beach right away!" Mr. Jones from next door said, "It's your nephew!"

"What is it? Is my son all right?" Aunt Millie bolted immediately.

"He's fine now. Thanks to young Greg."

"My Anthony..." Aunt Mildred was quivering.

Aunt Mildred and Uncle Willy were the first ones out the door, immediately followed by Jack and Warren. Dottie's dad and Aunt Audrey were directly behind them. Dottie's mother lingered behind to conclude her negotiations with Kate. When Dottie slipped out ahead of her, that vice grip closed in on her arm.

"Where do you think you're going?"

"To see Tony."

"No, you're not. I told you to stay out of people's way when we're on holiday. You stay here with Kate. There's nothing you can do for Tony."

"I want to be with him!"

"You'll just be in the way."

"But, Mom..."

"No, Dottie."

Excluded, shut out once again. Her mother did not release her arm until she was back in house, and slammed the door in her face.

"You heard her, kid." Kate had one leg slung over the armrest of the sagging sofa, "Stay put and don't bug me."

Dottie racked her brains for an escape plan. There had to be a way for her to slip out, undetected. She scoped out the kitchen. The back door was in full view of Her Majesty, as engrossed as she might be in her copy of Cosmopolitan magazine.

"Hey, kid!" she called out, cracking her gum, "Don't be getting up to anything out there!"

"I think I'll go up and read." she announced, "There's nothing to do down there."

"Yeah, you do that, kid."

Upstairs, Dottie climbed out to the fire escape from the bathroom window and slithered down the rusty metal ladder to the vacant lot, undetected by prying eyes. Her heart was pounding in fear of being detected by strangers who might mistake her for a burglar in her denim overalls and canvas unisex hat, scrawny enough to be mistaken for a boy.

A crowd was gathered on the beach, obscuring her view. As she drew closer, she saw his handsome, bronzed

51

body sprawled out on the sand, seaweed clinging to his dark curls...She ran to his side and knelt beside him, caressing his wet hair. Jack and Warren were attempting to engage his attention. Aunt Mildred was being comforted by Aunt Audrey and Dottie's mother. Uncle Willy and Dottie's father stood uncomfortably.

"He came out of nowhere and just walked into the water." someone in the crowd was saying.

"He seemed terribly preoccupied." said another, "In his own world."

"Dorothy Hope! What in the world! Didn't I tell you to stay at the house?" her mother's shrill voice rang out, drowning out other voices, "How did you manage to hoodwink Kate into letting you out?"

Dottie thought about how funny her mom looked with her hair in metal curlers out in public, not coiffed to perfection in the elaborately teased styles of the day. How embarrassed she must be, to be seen when not at her best! Her mother would later console herself that, at least, no one in Beavertown had seen her this way.

Dottie sat picking at the olive green seaweed covering Tony's chest, with centers like the bubble wrap inside packing envelopes.

"Young lady, you disobeyed me! I told you to stay home!"

"Annette..." Warren intercepted, "She's very close to Tony. Did you really think you could keep her away?"

A disoriented Tony stirred, opened his eyes and glanced around him in terror.

"It's okay, Tony." Dottie stroked his cheek.

He looked up and smiled at her. Her hand clasped his firmly. Nearby, Greg was surrounded by female admirers of all ages, mostly teens. He called out to her:

"Hey, Debbie! I hope your cousin's okay!"

"Thank you for giving Tony back to us."

"It's okay. Take it easy, Debbie." he returned to his groupies, "Man, I could've sworn there was someone with me, carrying him ashore. It was right creepy, man."

"I saw a woman's figure in the water, fully dressed." a middle-aged woman in the group said, "Then, she...just kind of vanished...Poof! I thought I was hallucinating."

"I saw her, too." another woman said, "She was all dressed in grey. Her hair was long."

Dottie's eyes met Jack's, who frowned knowingly. Tony's late wife had reached out to him from another realm to give his life back to him.

"Adele was here." Tony spoke, "She was pulling me out, before the lifeguard even got there."

"She was trying to tell you it wasn't your time yet." Jack said, his hand clasping Tony's shoulder.

"Was she really here?"

"Yes, she was. She's watching over you, Tony." Dottie said, "She knew she was needed and she let you know you're not alone."

When they returned home, Kate's cherry red suitcases were lined up by the door.

"Kate!" Jack called into the house in panic.

She appeared, dressed in her singular garment that covered her body: A psychedelic-print sundress.

"Kate, what's this?"

"I'm leaving, Jack. You can go back in one of the other cars. I'm taking the Mustang."

"You can't leave!"

"Can't I? Watch me. I've had it up to here with your psycho family and you! You're a wimp and a loser, Jack Chandler!"

"Kate..."

"Let her go, pal." Warren said, "She's not worth it. She's got the morals of an alley cat."

"You ought to know!" she retorted, her nostrils flaring, "It takes one to know one! You're the talk of this village, with your midnight dalliances!"

"Kate, please, let's talk about this!" Jack blocked her way.

"There's nothing more to say, Jack. It's over. Good-bye, Mama's Boy." she stormed out.

"Let's celebrate." Warren smirked, "Jack's a free man again! I hope she took her cat-of-nine-tails and her handcuffs with her."

Her arms still around Tony's waist, Dottie wondered why it was that the family had accepted Kate into the fold, albeit with reservations, yet not Brett. Dottie had always been fond of Brett and would have been hard-pressed to find any faults. Kate, on the other hand, was a different story. Aunt Audrey was apparently far more broad-minded than Aunt Mildred and Uncle Willy.

The following morning, Dottie awoke before the others and walked down to the beach with "Death On The Nile". Few people inhabited the sand at such an early hour.

By midmorning, young families with boisterous children arrived, making their presence known. A black poodle frolicked and played fetch with blonde-headed humans, barking in an irritating pitch. The sun shimmered on the water, dotted with red inflatable balls. Dottie sent her dreams out to sea, to destinations unknown, far, far away.

"What's Poirot up to?" Warren was reading over her shoulder.

"I wish I could put all my stories on paper. I wish I had words to breathe life into my imaginings."

"Why don't you try? I'll get you some notebooks and those pens with green ink that you're so crazy about."

"Aw, you've got to have red ink for a murder mystery!"

"Of course! How silly of me!"

"I have no talent, Warren. I can't even get a passing grade in English class! Mrs. Ellis hates me."

"What does she know?"

"You're the literary one in the family, Warren. You should write a book about all of us."

"It would be banned in nine provinces, except Quebec."

A smile crept across her face for the first time.

"How's Tony?" she said, once again solemn, "Is he up yet?"

"He was up listening to Tony Bennett. I sat through "Boulevard Of Broken Dreams", "Once Upon A Time", "Who Can I Turn To?" and three repeats of "Stranger In Paradise". I couldn't take any more."

"When we get back home, I'm going to see Brett and try to get those two back together."

"You're an incurable romantic."

"I can't say I'm sorry to see the last of Kate, though. I never liked her."

"The witch finally flew the coop." Warren mused, chewing on a piece of tall grass, "I don't know why he ever married that Trollope."

"He thought he loved her."

"Love." he laughed, "What is love, but an illusion?"

"You're so cynical."

"It's an invitation to being exploited and played for a fool." he tossed the chewed-up blade of grass into the thicket.

"Warren, no one can ever play you for a fool. You're always in control. You call all the shots."

"Don't think, Shortstuff, that, if I ever let my guard down for an instant, there wouldn't be a bevy of opportunistic females ready to pounce on me and suck the life out of me." he smiled sardonically, his deep dimples settling into permanence.

"Warren, that's really sad."

"And you, Shortstuff...You need to grow another layer of skin. Young men are going to be buzzing around you when they catch a whiff of Horncastle money."

"Even our family money won't make me attractive. That's one thing you don't have to worry about."

"Mark my words: It will."

"I know you were burned by Sharon, but she was loony tunes. She was obsessive. Not all women are like her. Don't seal your heart shut so that you can't open it again."

"They're all the same: Clingy, manipulative, devious...Do you know how many times I've been playing that tape in my mind over and over? If I had only returned home earlier...Nina would be alive today."

"Warren, you need to let it go and forgive yourself. What happened was not your fault. You had no way of knowing what Sharon was capable of."

"Nina believed her when she told her I was leaving her to marry Sharon. She took that entire bottle of pills. If I had only arrived a little earlier...She might still be alive today."

"You haven't allowed yourself to get that emotionally close to anyone else after Nina died. You haven't given yourself permission to be that vulnerable since."

"If Jack has any sense, he'll cut that conniving gold-digger Kate out of his life without a cent. Women like that have a radar for vulnerable men. They know how to push the right buttons, how to get what they want."

"All nice people – men or women – get used and hurt."

"That's why I'm such an asshole."

"Is that really the answer, Warren?"

"Get them before they get you. Words to live by."

"Don't you ever worry about being alone in your old age?"

"There are no guarantees, Shortstuff. Tony married Adele. We all thought they'd grow old together. Who imagined she would get cancer and die so young?"

"Tony took a risk and fell in love again. This time, the family got in his way."

"Look where it got him. He nearly lost his life. Is it really worth it?"

"Mr. No Commitment. One of these days, you're going to fall very hard."

"Not a chance. I stay away from the 'nice' girls. I don't want to be a total jerk." he rose and brushed the sand off his shorts.

"I would still like to believe there's some hope, some possibility of happiness for nice folks."

"I hope, for you, there is. I hope you have special angels watching over you."

"We all have angels."

"How did you get to be so smart, huh?" he tugged at her ponytail.

"I'm an outcast. All outcasts are blessed with wisdom to compensate for their social ineptitude."

"You took after Audrey. She's the only sane one in the family. Willy and Don are anal retentive stuffed shirts; Frances thinks all laws are made to be broken; I'm a pompous ass because I'm the baby of the family and not much older than my nephews."

"It's nice to have a young swinger for an uncle."

"You're my only fan."

"And you, mine. We should stick together."

"Just try to get rid of me."

"Never."

"You're good for my ego, Shortstuff."

"Warren, do you think Aunt Audrey'll remarry? It's been a long time since Uncle Ted died."

"If she's smart, she won't."

She punched him playfully in the arm. She wished it could always be like this: Lazy summer days stretching endlessly into shimmering warm nights; Warren, Tony and Jack by her side, no worries about school, being suspended in time with no winter in sight.

"Aunt Mildred kept vigil by Tony's bedside all night. I heard her crying through the wall."

"He has it bad...Poor old schmuck."

"It was nice of you to bunk with Jack last night, so she could stay with Tony."

"Jack would have preferred someone with more curves, but he had to settle for me."

"Jack's being very brave for Tony's sake. He's hiding his own pain."

"He's been down this road before many, many times. He's a chick magnet for all the wrong chicks. Every cent he earns goes to his multiple alimony cheques."

"He's gorgeous. But he's unfortunately also sweet and sensitive. Deadly combination. Recipe for heartbreak."

"You're learning from all of our foolish mistakes. Hey, Shortstuff, what about a chili dog?"

"Um. No, thanks." she lowered her eyes.

He scanned the group of teenagers congregated outside the canteen, smoking and sharing private jokes.

"Are they bothering you?"

"These locals aren't nearly as bad as the kids back home."

"Teenagers are a strange breed, I must admit."

"I don't know how you can stand teaching them. I'd never want to be a teacher. I'd feel like throttling the obnoxious brats!"

"It's not so bad once you get used to them."

"I could never get used to them...I don't want to go back to school. It's so depressing to settle back into the same old rut."

"Come on. Let's get a couple of chili dogs at the canteen. I'll protect you."

She complied. They walked the narrow path up to the grey wooden shack. Girls beside the Coke vending machine snickered.

"There's Miss Priss in her white shorts!"

"Who's the dreamboat with her? Her dad?"

"Nah. He's not old enough to be her dad. He's too cool."

"He looks like a movie star!" a mouse-faced nymphet with a long sheet of light brown hair concealing her eyes sighed.

"Shh. I think he is." a pudgy blonde covered the other one's mouth.

"Sally, you dummy! What would a movie star be doing here, in this neck of the woods? He'd be in Hollywood."

"He's a Canadian movie star, dufus! He's like, the best looking guy I've ever seen!"

"Let's get his autograph!"

"Yeah – let's get his autograph! Some day, he'll be the next Paul Newman and we can tell people we knew him when he was practically an unknown!" a third girl, shorter than the other two, chimed in.

"Miss Priss just called him Warren. I've never heard of any movie stars named Warren except Warren Beatty."

"That's his disguise, stupid. He wants to go 'incoherent'. You know, like, he doesn't want people to know who he is."

"Cathy, you dope! That's 'incongruous'!"

"No. That's 'incognito', girls." Warren shot back a wink, leaving them breathless and flushed, "And, by the way, I don't give autographs."

Warren and Dottie brushed past them, chili dogs in hand.

"They really think you're a movie star!" Dottie chuckled.

"They must be blind, as well as stupid."

"You're better looking than all the movie stars."

"Flattery will get you an ice cream cone at the Dairy Bar after lunch." he winked, "I don't think those kids are going to be bothering you anymore."

"They wouldn't dare mess with a movie star's niece!"

"I'm surprised they haven't mobbed Jack – mistaken him for Robert Redford."

"Maybe they haven't seen him. Kate kept him on a short leash."

"He'd better watch out now. He's the only real celebrity around here. I can't believe someone somewhere hasn't recognized him. Don't they sell any records in this one horse hick town?"

"His music only appeals to a select few. Most people listen to deafening rock music. My generation's totally uncouth, not to mention tone-deaf."

"You were born old, Shortstuff." he tousled her hair, "You're more mature, astute and wise than all of us."

"Thank you." she squeezed his arm.

Discarding their paper napkins in the orange waste receptacle, they climbed the hill arm in arm to the Dairy Bar.

Upon their return home, Dottie felt renewed relief at not seeing Kate's surly face. Jack and Tony were alone in the living room playing backgammon and listening to Tony Bennett. Her mother and aunts were occupied with dishes and supper preparations. Their kitchen radio was blaring out its tinny rendition of "Feeling Groovy", ludicrously clashing with Tony Bennett's "Tender Is The Night". Her father and Uncle Willy were on the back porch, reading the local newspaper and discussing the stock market, the cacophony of their voices a familiar drone. With Kate out of the picture, perhaps, they could now spend what remained of this vacation in peace.

"Dottie, peel the potatoes for supper!" her mother bellowed.

"What's in the bag?" Aunt Audrey noticed the paper bag Warren was holding.

"Freshly baked dinner rolls from the bakery. Shortstuff and I took a big walk."

"We assumed as much, seeing as neither one of you showed up for lunch." Dottie's mother shot up a glance at them.

"How lovely." Aunt Audrey took the bag from Warren and peeked in, "Don was at the fish market and brought back a treasure trove of culinary delights. We'll be dining in style tonight."

Dottie peeked into one of the stock pots boiling on the stove.

"Neat! I love scorpions!"

"They're not scorpions, dear." Aunt Audrey stifled a laugh, "They're lobsters."

"I couldn't think of the name. All those creepy things look alike to me."

"Those 'creepy things' are delicacies." her mother said.

"With the exception of scorpions." Warren winked.

"Get to work, Dottie." her mother commanded, "Millie, Audrey and I are going out to the shops. We need to alleviate some stress. You and the boys can get supper on. You do the potatoes; they'll help with the salad. The seafood's already boiling. Watch them closely, so they don't boil over. Warren knows when it's done."

"Warren, I'll be fine on my own. You go in and relax with the guys." Dottie reassured him once the ladies were gone.

"Are you sure?"

"I'm positive." she shut off the radio in order to hear Tony Bennett's record.

When they all sat down for supper, a stony silence surrounded them. The only words spoken consisted of "Pass the butter, please." and "Thank you".

Dottie scanned their stoic faces, twirling her fork like a baton.

"Dorothy Hope," her mother glared, "Stop playing with your cutlery."

Aunt Mildred picked at her food like a nervous robin.

"This meal is superb." her father remarked congenially, "You ladies really outdid yourselves."

"Dottie's the one who deserves credit." Jack said.

"It's really good." Tony said weakly.

"Thanks, guys."

"Tony, dear," Aunt Mildred said, "Why don't you take an extended holiday so you can travel through Europe for a couple of months? France must be lovely in autumn."

"April in Paris!" Dottie's mother broke into song, giggling.

Too much white wine, thought Dottie.

"Continental women are very beautiful." her dad simpered.

"Yes, dear," Aunt Mildred lit up, "You'll meet someone new in no time."

"You need to throw yourself into your work more." Uncle Willy remarked, "You need to keep busy, so you'll have no time or energy to think about that gold-digger. It's not healthy to have too much time on your hands."

Oblivious to the series of monologues directed at himself, the pale Tony kept his eyes lowered and fidgeted with his napkin.

"Brett's not a gold-digger!" Dottie's voice pierced the icy silence.

Cold glares were promptly directed in her direction from her parents and the iron couple. Astounded by her own courage, intoxicated by the power of her words, she sprang to her feet.

"You guys think you have all the answers, don't you? Just listen to all of you: Stuff it in, deny it, sweep it under the rug! No one speaks from the heart! You're so caught up in what other people think, you don't even know who you are or what matters anymore. You're all robots. And you hate anyone who is real, who has feelings, who's not perfect! You hate that Tony and Jack and I are different; we don't live up to your superficial expectations. We can't be callous and phony. We're real and honest and we have feelings. That makes us every parent's nightmare."

No one spoke when she paused to catch her breath.

"If Tony and Brett are in love, what business is it of anyone else's? What right do any of you have to look down your noses at Brett or anyone else? What makes you think you're so much better? Your money? Does money buy the ticket to entitlement? What right do any of you have to interfere in Tony's life?"

"That's quite enough, Dorothy Hope." her father said coldly.

The exhilaration of emotional release promptly turned to horror.

"This hysterical outburst is not appropriate behavior, young lady!" her mother flung the words at her, with eyes like two wooden beads.

"You need to have a better reign on your emotions, dear." Aunt Mildred buzzed like a mosquito.

"At least, I'm not a hypocrite like the rest of you!" Dottie shot back; she could not stop now – or she might burst.

"Mind your manners, young lady. We did not raise you to be so impertinent."

"All you care about is what your friends think! You judge people by how they present themselves on the surface, not by what's in their souls!"

"You're emotionally immature for your age." her dad said, "You need to do a lot of growing up. When you do, you'll learn to respect the rules of civilized society and you'll be able to co-exist with people. It takes some people longer to reach emotional maturity. You've led such a pampered life, your perspective is warped. You haven't experienced enough hardship, enough struggle."

"What would you know? You don't know me! None of you know me, or Tony, or Jack! You don't even know yourselves! You tell us how to dress, how to behave, how to conduct our personal lives, what to do for a living, whom to marry, whom to vote for, what functions to attend. Everything is decided for us. We are not allowed to have our own minds, opinions, tastes, feelings. We're not allowed to talk about anything that actually matters. We're even told when to use the bathroom."

"That's quite enough, Dorothy!" her dad roared, "Go to your room!"

"Go easy, Don." Warren said.

"This is none of your concern, Warren." her mother chided him, "You don't have children of your own, so you're not in a position to tell us how to raise ours."

"Go to your room, young lady!" her dad roared again.

"With pleasure!" she bounded up the stairs.

"Don, dear, watch your blood pressure." she could hear her mother.

"She's a spitfire." Uncle Willy said.

"She's overemotional." Aunt Mildred said, "Takes everything to heart."

"She's totally irrational." her mother said.

"She's a no-hoper." this was her father, "She'll never amount to anything."

"I have a good mind to go up there and have it out with her." her mother's shrill voice ran out.

"No Annette." Aunt Audrey, who had been silent throughout the entire episode, spoke for the first time, "She needs time alone. She needs her space."

"What that girl needs is a military school for girls." her father said.

In her room, Dottie stuffed her necessary items of clothing into her overnight bag haphazardly, squashed them down to make room for Alfie, her teddy bear. She zipped it with difficulty and slung the long thick strap across her chest to distribute its weight evenly. The fire escape was familiar territory to her by now.

The beach was darker than ever under the anemic crescent moon. In her favorite spot, she removed her teddy bear and her grey bulky cardigan from her bag. The night time temperatures in Maine did not dip down to the extremes they were accustomed to back home, however, she still shuddered in the night chill. In a secluded spot concealed by thick bushes, she deposited her bag and settled into a reclining position, placing her head on it. It would have to do for one night. Tomorrow, she would have to pilfer a pillow and a blanket from the house when everyone was out. Clutching Alfie to her chest, she curled up in a fetal position. She would spend the night here and think about her options in the daylight. Somehow, things always seemed more hopeful in the sunlight. She shut her eyes and drifted off to sleep.

She did not know what it was that awoke her: The rustling of the leaves in the bushes, or the distant howling of dogs. No derelicts or teenagers were known to frequent this stretch of the beach at nights. Perhaps, it was a grizzly in search of food. She had not brought food with her in her haste to make a quick exit. Did that mean she would have to be his snack? She held her breath and prayed he did not find her. Then, she heard distinctly human footsteps. She was not going to be eaten, but a fate far worse awaited her: She was about to be robbed and beaten. The only item of monetary value on her was her silver charm bracelet, with all the zodiac charms for each member of the family: Scorpio for Warren; Pisces for Jack and herself, Cancer for Tony; Virgo for Aunt Audrey; Libra for her mom; Gemini for her dad; Leo for Uncle Willy; Aquarius for Aunt Mildred. And, she still had the two Taurus charms for Adele and Ella who were no longer of this world. A hand reached from behind her and covered her mouth and nose. She could not breathe.

"Don't make a sound."

What was he doing here? Was he trying to make a point about her inability to fend for herself in the world? Was this just another cruel adult scheme to break her will?

A sour-smelling tea towel replaced the hand over her mouth, and a necktie over it to fasten it behind her. He bound her hands behind her with twine. Moaning and writhing, she attempted to break free, however, he overpowered her, exhaling alcohol-soaked breath on her face. Crushed under his enormous weight, she slipped into dark oblivion...

She was jolted back to consciousness by a stabbing pain – an unfamiliar pain – in her lower regions. Clammy skin on her own skin alerted her to the fact that her jeans and underpants had been lowered to her ankles. Immobilized by terror, she watched him being pulled off herself. She could hear punches being thrown, groans and muffled swearing. The shadows drifted outside her field of vision. Then, she heard that familiar voice:

"Fuck you! You fucking bastard!"

And, the struggle was over. Her attacker had been defeated. Her rescuer removed her gag and untied her.

"It's all right. I'm here now. That son of a bitch can never hurt you again." he pulled her close and kissed the top of her head.

"I thought I was dead."

"You're going to be all right." he pushed her hair out of her face, "Let's get you to a doctor."

"No! No doctor!"

"You need to be examined."

"This is a small town. Everyone'll find out."

"I'll take you to a doctor in Ellsworth. People don't know us there. There's a lady doctor there that I know. She'll do it as a favor to me. I'll call on her at her home." He turned his back to allow her privacy in getting dressed, "From there, I'll take you home."

She zipped up her jeans and pulled down her long cardigan. Her thighs were sticky and sore from being forced open. He brushed the sand off her face, hair and clothing. He picked up her teddy bear and shoulder bag.

"Get into my car and keep the doors locked. I'll get Tony and Jack from the house." He led her to his black Mercedes Benz parked at the far end of the path leading to the house, threw her bag in the trunk, unlocked the door on the passenger's side and reached in to open the back door. She climbed into the back seat. He handed Alfie to her and wrapped her in the woolen blanket beside her. She reached for his wrist.

"What if he does this again?" she uttered in terror.

"Not as long as I'm alive. I've got the goods on the mother fucker. He knows, if he goes anywhere near you, I'll beat the crap out of him. No one can hurt you, as long as I'm around, Dottie."

"Warren – I love you."

"And, I love you."

"What are you going to tell Tony and Jack?"

"That you've got food poisoning. This will be our secret."

"Thank you."

"I don't think Tony's ready to find out what a bastard his father really is. Stay tight. I'll be back with the boys."

Warren – the keeper of secrets...She pulled the blanket up to her chin.

Tony was the first to arrive at the car, albeit sans luggage. He knocked groggily on the window and she unlocked his side. He slid in beside her.

"Warren said the four of us are going back early. You don't feel well, he said."

"Some sort of food poisoning, I think. The worst is pretty well over now."

"I'm sorry, Dottie. We're stopping in Ellsworth, so you can get some medical attention."

"I'll be just fine, Tony. As soon as we get home, you're going to call Brett. Don't let the family ruin your life. Follow your heart. Brett loves you. I know she does. Marry her. You must promise me, Tony."

"You're priceless." he placed his arm around her shoulder.

Warren and Jack came bounding, carrying multiple suitcases and deposited them in the trunk.

"Okay, let's go!" Warren settled into the driver's seat, "Hold on tight! This rocket's sailing to the moon!"

Warren inserted an eight track tape into the player. Billy Vaughan And His Orchestra began playing "Wheels".

"No more Tony Bennett." Warren said, "You wore the poor guy out, pal. He needs a break."

Jack winked at the two of them in the back seat. Tony smiled weakly.

"How are the others all going to squeeze into Don's car?" Jack turned to Warren.

"Brother Willy and Mildred are just going to have to squeeze into the back seat with your mother, Jacko. That Lincoln Continental will seat five comfortably."

"I think Mom heard us thrashing around upstairs but she never said a word."

"Audrey's all right. Old Millie Dear slept like a log the whole time I was packing Tony's bag right under her nose. She snored like a chainsaw. In the morning, she'll shriek: 'Where's my Tony? Where's my son? He's been abducted by UFOs!'" he spoke in a high-pitched voice.

"I don't think Mom's going to say a word to her or anyone else." Jack said.

"She won't."

In this car full of wounded souls, Dottie rested her head on Tony's shoulder and shut her eyes. Sheltered from the world, surrounded by the ones she cherished most, she knew she was safe and wanted. All was well with the world – so long as Warren and her two cousins were with her. Warren turned off the eight track and switched to the radio to listen to the news. Maureen McGovern's song "The Morning After" was playing before the news came on. At that blissful moment, she had no way of knowing that this was to be the final time the four of them would be together. Dottie's predictable existence had come to a crashing halt during that final holiday at the summer rental in Maine. No one returned to the beach house. In subsequent years, summers were spent in splintered groups at the family's lakeside cottage in Nova Scotia. Dottie had no way of knowing on that warm August night that, some day, she would have to choose one of her loved ones over another, that her family would become torn apart, with her Warren at the center of every controversy. He and Jack were never to be co-conspirators or tennis partners or friends again. And no one was ever to speak of the summer of '72.

Chapter 7/ YESTERDAY WHEN I WAS YOUNG

Oversized snowflakes were whirling in a hypnotizing dance around the Victorian lamppost on the corner. A beat-up once-white taxi pulled up in front of the house to let out its lone female passenger, and drove off in a cloud of snow. The woman slowly and deliberately made her way up the porch steps. Inhaling the crisp cold air deeply, she rang the doorbell. The air smelled pure as a virgin forest in the hush of a winter night. All the lights were on inside the house: Someone had to be home. The curtain on the small square pain of glass in the door parted and the door opened tentatively to reveal the tall, middle-aged woman. In her dark print caftan and bifocals, she appeared deceptively non-threatening, not at all like the femme fatale she was known to be. Faint recognition spread across her face and her jaw dropped in disbelief.

"Miss Morrow, I'm sure you don't know me. My name is Lea Norbert." she spoke rapidly, afraid to lose her nerve.

"I know who you are. Why don't you step inside, Lea? It's a nasty night out there."

Lea reluctantly stepped into the foyer.

"Come in. Sit down." Brett motioned toward the living room, "Would you like some hot chocolate to warm up?"

"I don't want to be any trouble." Lea stood awkwardly.

"May I take your coat?" Brett offered, arms outstretched.

"No, thank you."

"Have a seat. I don't bite."

Lea blushed and unbuttoned her royal blue wool tent coat to expose her protruding abdomen. Brett's eyes, even more enormous now, fell on this unexpected sight.

"It's Tony's."

Brett was speechless.

"He doesn't know."

"How...How far along?"

"Five months.."

"You haven't told him. Yet you have told me."

"You see, I know Tony doesn't love me. He never has. You are the only woman he has ever loved. I had to meet you myself to try to understand the Brett Morrow mystique. I would like to know how you turn grown men into putty."

"Lea, things are not always the way they seem."

"You are very beautiful. I knew from the start, I could never compete with you. Tony's always going to love you."

"I haven't seen Tony for a very long time." she glanced at Lea's abdomen.

"Tony and I are not together anymore. He dumped me in July. He has turned his sights to a younger woman. They say her father is going to be the next premier of New Brunswick."

"Lea, I don't know what to say, treasure. Please have a seat." she took Lea's coat from her and hung it up on the hall rack, "I'll make us some hot chocolate. Do you like marshmallows?"

"Yes." Lea followed her into the kitchen.

"Tony has to be told." Brett spoke matter-of-factly, "He has to live up to his obligations."

"I don't want him to feel he has to marry me. I don't want any man to marry me unless he loves me and only me. If he finds out I'm pregnant, he might resent me and feel tied down. He might think I wasn't careful enough."

"It takes two to make a baby – and birth control should be a shared responsibility."

"I was raised in a strict Catholic home. I'm not very experienced. I didn't know things would progress to that level, so I was unprepared. I thought it was a safe time of the month. I guess I was wrong. I think he would be very upset if he knew."

"Men! They want all the pleasure, none of the responsibility! Why didn't he take responsibility for birth control?"

"It's the woman's responsibility."

"In this day and age, I can't believe men are still getting away with that one! They've got all women brainwashed! And women just lap up all the bull! I think women must unite and refuse to put up with it!" Brett said indignantly, "Souls are getting damaged in today's sexual merry-go-round. I hate to see you hurting like this, Lea."

"This is not at all the reaction I expected from you, Brett."

"What did you expect, hon?" Brett poured boiling water into the mugs and stirred the concoction; its sweet aroma tantalizing Lea.

"I thought you might be resentful...where it's Tony's baby..."

"I have no claims on Tony. He's a free agent."

"You don't think of me as a threat because I'm not attractive."

"Lea, darling!" Brett embraced her, "It's nothing like that! Don't ever think that!"

"You've been really nice to me."

"Nice? Not too many people would describe me that way." she smoothed Lea's hair, "Are you hungry? Let me fix us a snack."

"Don't go to any trouble."

"It's no trouble. I'm hungry myself. Egg salad on oatmeal bread okay?"

"Sure."

"I stay away from white bread. It's bad for you. Pull up a chair, hon. Put your feet up on another. Once I'm done making the sandwiches, we can eat them in the living room where it's more comfortable."

"You're doing all this for me?"

"You are with child. That entitles you to being treated like a queen. Do you have family nearby, Lea?"

"My whole family's in Bathurst."

"Any close friends?"

She shook her head.

"You can't go through this pregnancy alone." Brett cut the sandwiches in triangles and placed them on Corelle plates.

"A lot of people do. Single women with poor judgment do."

"That's nonsense. We'll get through this together. As a team." she removed a plastic container from her fridge and decorated the plates with celery and carrot sticks.

"I can see why Tony loves you very much. How could he not?" Lea's misty eyes met Brett's own.

"There. Our snack's ready. Come on, hon." she led the way back to the living room, carrying both plates; she propped Lea up with pillows and provided a footstool for her.

Lea's eyes scrutinized her surroundings: The understated elegance of the peach upholstered furniture, the red Oriental carpet, the paintings of nudes hanging on the walls, the rosewood antique piano with sheet music scattered around it, the dried and silk puffballs of hydrangea and cream-colored oleander in oversized glass and ceramic vases. The books in the mahogany bookcases appeared to be works by famous American playwrights from a more gracious era.

"Do you live alone, Lea?"

"Yes."

"I hope you don't have a lot of stairs to climb."

"I'm on the second floor of a house on Montgomery Street. There are outdoor stairs to my apartment. The owner lives downstairs."

"Those steps must be awfully slippery in winter. Sounds like the second floor was added later on, if it's only accessible from outside."

"I've never thought about it before. It's such an adorable 1950's style house. It's painted candy pink. Everyone knows it, too. People just call it 'the pink house'."

"I'm worried about the stairs, hon. You need to be extra careful now. If you don't mind my asking, how old are you, Lea?"

"Thirty-nine."

Both were well aware this might be Lea's only chance to have a child.

"I think the Horncastles owe you accommodations. After all, you're going to bring another Horncastle into the world."

"Oh, no...I wouldn't want them to know about this."

"Tony has to know. I think I'll call him now and ask him to come over."

"Do you think that's wise?" Lea's eyes grew wide.

"Sweetheart, he is just as responsible for this new life as you."

"I know you're right. I just dread the thought of breaking the news to him. Especially now that he's dating Alexandra Clark."

"He has to be told sooner or later. Do you want him to hear about it from someone else?"

"People think I'm just getting fatter. At work, they've been remarking on all the weight I've been putting on, but no one has suspected Lea Norbert, Miss Goody-Two-Shoes could ever be an unwed mother."

"That's unidimensional thinking on their part. No one fits one singular stereotypical image. Human beings cannot be pigeon-holed. We all have various components. I have a puritanical side and you have a bon-vivant side. We're all searching for fulfillment, but most of us have to look in the wrong places first before we can find the right ones. Some of us never do. I've already missed the boat."

"You mean Tony?"

"Not Tony. I let him go a long time ago."

"That's what I have to do now: Let him go. Isn't that what love is all about?"

"Oh, sweetness…" Brett reached across to pat her on the arm.

"You're right. I need to tell him. It might be easier with you here. Otherwise, I might chicken out."

"Good girl. I'll call him now." she placed her plate on the coffee table and sprang up.

While Brett was in the kitchen, Lea devoured her sandwich and the strips of carrot and celery on the plate.

"He's on his way over." Brett announced as she returned.

"Please don't leave me alone with him."

"I'll be right by your side, hon."

"Thank you. I've been thinking about Natural Childbirth. It's not that common around here yet, but I think it's the best way to go. It's going to be the way of the future. And, I want to breast-feed. I know formula feeding is de rigeur right now, but I think breast-feeding is best. What do you think?"

"I breast-fed all my babies until they were six months old, but I had to supplement with formula, as well. I didn't produce enough milk. But I believe, the longer you can breast-feed, the better."

"With four children, you'd know. I'm sorry, I knew about your children because Tony told me. I asked him. I was curious about you. Mystified. I wanted to know about the beautiful Brett Morrow. I think it's amazing that you have so many children. You must know all there is to know about motherhood."

"Not necessarily, hon. We all make mistakes."

"I'm staying away from tea and coffee, and I'm not touching a drop of wine."

"Even while breast-feeding, because it still gets passed on through the milk. I know people would never believe this, but during all four of my pregnancies, I did not touch a drop of alcohol, didn't take any medications, prescribed or over the counter. I didn't smoke or ingest caffeine. When you're pregnant or breast-feeding, the welfare of that child becomes your utmost concern."

"People don't really know you, Brett. This is a side of you they don't even know exists. They only see the public image you present."

"It's best that they don't know me."

"I don't think so. I'm glad I had this glimpse into your true self."

"You're very kind. How does your family feel about your condition?"

"They don't approve."

"Give them time. They'll get used to it. Once they see that tiny little treasure, they'll have a change of heart."

"I was hoping Mom would come down during the third trimester and stay with me, go to Lamaze with me as my coach. But it's just not to be."

"Have you picked a coach in her place?"

"No. I don't know anyone that well."

"If you like, I can be your coach."

"You'd do that for me?"

"Of course."

They heard a car coming to a stop in front of the house.

"Must be Tony." Brett rose, "You okay, hon?"

"I'm as composed as I'll ever be."

"Hang in there, baby." Brett unfurled her long legs and headed to the foyer to open the door before he had time to ring the bell.

"Hi, beautiful. What's this big surprise you have for me?" Tony stood smiling.

"Please come in." she directed him matter-of-factly.

At the sight of Lea, he froze and looked from one to the other.

"I believe you two have met." Brett said.

"Is this a joke of some sort?" he glared accusingly.

"Don't be so paranoid, darling."

"Lea, what are you doing here?"

"We're good friends." Brett sat beside Lea and took her hand in her own.

"Since when?" Tony eyed them with suspicion.

"Since earlier tonight. There's something you need to know: In a little over four months, you're going to be a daddy." Brett announced.

Tony appeared perplexed.

"Don't look so distressed." Lea finally spoke, "I don't want anything from you. I only agreed to let you know because Brett said I should."

"How did this happen?"

"You were there, hon." Brett said, "You ought to know."

"I thought you took precautions."

"Nothing is foolproof."

"We'll get married right away."

"Tony, I don't want you to marry me because you feel obligated. I don't want to tie you down."

"Why didn't you tell me before?"

"I didn't tell anyone."

"You told Brett before anyone else? I don't understand."

"She and I have something in common."

"It's not safe for Lea to be climbing those outdoor stairs to her apartment." Brett said, "I think she needs alternate accommodations. Don't you have some unoccupied suites at your house?"

"Well...er...There's Aunt Audrey's old suite."

"This is all making my head spin." Lea said.

"You can stay here tonight." Brett said, "I have spare nighties, toothbrushes, lotions, towels. Those stairs must be awfully slippery on a cold night like this."

"I haven't given my landlord my month's notice."

"Don't worry about that." Tony offered, "I'll talk to him. I'll find a tenant for him, and pay him next month's rent myself."

"Thank you. Both of you are very kind."

"There's a new life inside you and we all owe it to that fragile, innocent creature to provide the best care possible."

"Thank you." Lea embraced Brett.

Brett fought back her tears. Lea had presented her with the opportunity to redeem herself. But, perhaps it was already too late.

Chapter 8/ ENDINGS

On the phonograph, Eileen Farrell was singing "You're Nearer". Sydney placed the rectangular red biscuit tin on the coffee table and opened it to reveal bundles of postcards, letters and Polaroid snapshots tied with pink satin ribbons. She deftly removed the postcard at the top of one bundle and turned it over to read it. The date on it was April 27th, 1978 – two years from their first meeting and one year from his return to Beavertown from the world tour...Long before they were lovers...

"Hi, Sydney. Greetings from Vancouver. I'm at the legendary Sylvia Hotel! Would you believe the original owner's name was Goldstein? He named it after his daughter in 1913. Did you know my mother's name was Sylvia? Had she lived, I know she would have loved you. She was kind and nurturing like you. I think of her every day and miss her terribly. She died when I was thirteen, and though I've been calling Audrey 'Mom' since she married Dad, no one can be my mom except Sylvia Chandler. By the way, as it turns out, Sylvia Hotel boasted Vancouver's earliest cocktail lounge in 1954. I think these coincidences are not mere coincidences. You and I have some sort of cosmic connection..."

She also wished Sylvia were still living. She would have accepted her. From all the things Jack had told her, she could tell Sylvia had not possessed a snobbish or devious bone in her body, unlike Audrey. Who knew what Audrey had done to Jack, and where she had spirited him away?

It was time to accept the fact that she might never see Jack again. In three days, it would be 1981. She needed to release him with love and pray he was safe and happy wherever he was. Their roles in each other's lives had ended.

They had been destined to share only a brief period of time. She needed to accept this fact and close the chapter. It was time to move on.

The telephone rang. She closed the tin and caressed the top of it before reaching for the receiver.

"Hi, Syd." It was Tony.

"Hi, Tony." she wiped away a tear with her fingertip, "How are things in good old B.Town?"

"Dull as ever. How are things in Toronto?"

"Same as ever."

"The reason I called you is, I need your feedback about some of the work being done on the Chandler building."

"I would be happy to give feedback, but, Tony, I was going to call you about that...I would like to ask you to buy me out."

"Sydney..."

"I think it would be best if your family had no ties to me anymore. I'm sure you know what Jack likes, and I have complete confidence in you to create a masterpiece that would make him proud. This is best for everyone involved. I'll legally change my name back to Goldstein, as well."

"But..."

"I think we all know Jack is not coming back. No use prolonging this agony. All the leads have come up empty. He has vanished without a trace. He obviously doesn't wish to be found. We all need to move on."

"Whatever you wish...I'll draw up the papers. I'm sorry about all the pain this has caused you."

"Thank you."

"Are you still coming for the grand opening next November?"

"I'm not sure, Tony. We'll see. But I'll be there for Dottie's graduation this May."

"I hope you do decide to come for the opening, Syd. You've got a whole year to make a decision. I'll let you go now. We'll talk later. Thanks."

"Thanks, Tony."

She crossed the living room to the side table where a framed photo of Jack was smiling at her. She picked it up, returned to her seat, opened the tin and tucked the photo into it. Kissing the top of the tin, she whispered:

"Good-bye, my love."

* * *

"Mom?" the little voice on the other end said, "There's something I need to tell you. I hope you won't be too disappointed in me."

"I'd never be disappointed in you, sweetheart!" Brett reassured her, "No matter what it is, I'm fine with it."

"I'm leaving nursing school."

"It's about time!"

"That's a relief."

"I bit my tongue this past year, but I never felt that sham of a place was good enough for you. A treasure like you should never have to put up with that prison camp treatment from a bunch of back alley hags on a power trip."

"I'm so relieved, Mom."

"Just put that evil place behind you now."

"I will. Emerald keeps harassing me about being a loser and bringing shame upon them. She found out when I was sick with the flu a while back and Sam blurted it out. You're the first one I've told."

"That psycho woman needs a swift kick in the rear! Ignore her. You've wasted away to a skeleton at that place. No wonder you kept fainting. Just concentrate on getting your health back."

"Thank you, Mom."

"I'll come and visit you on the weekend, if it's all right with you two."

"All right? We'll be delighted!"

"Chuck's going to visit his uncle and said he can drive me."

"I can't wait."

"Me, too. We'll have to start putting some meat on your bones."

"I've just written a story about my most memorable week during the only rotation that mattered to me. I'd like to show it to you."

"I'd love to read it, sweetheart. What did you call it?"

"'The Final Week'. It's about my psychiatry rotation at Happy Valley."

"I can't wait to read it."

* * *

Ribby placed her orange plastic lunch tray on the table and sat down to savor her long-awaited lunch of open-faced hot turkey sandwich with peas, French fries, and gravy. She felt a soft tap on her shoulder.

"Sorry, I didn't mean to startle you."

Ribby turned around to find the demure, slender British nurse, whose name she could not recall. She was married to one of the urologists.

"I had to talk to you, Roberta." she took a seat at the table, "I know you're fond of that poor chap, Chad Johnson."

"I sure am." Ribby eyed her in anticipation; what was this woman's name? She wished she could remember.

"There's something that has been bothering me for quite a while, but I couldn't tell anyone. I know I can trust you."

"I appreciate that."

"I think we need to do something to help him." the woman lowered her voice, "There's something terribly wrong."

"I agree with you. I'm sorry, I can't think of your name."

"That's all right. It's Verity."

"Verity. It's a lovely name. You were saying something is terribly wrong."

"Yes. The woman with him claims to be his mother, yet she subjects him to Hollis Mazot's sadistic experiments. I have the feeling she doesn't want him to get better."

"She's a strange duck, that one."

"She seems to be hiding something. Chad did not have a memory problem when he first regained consciousness. I was assigned to him that night. He was persistently asking for someone named 'Sydney'. He told me that she was his wife and they had been injured in a fire. He asked me to find her. Just then, his mother walked in, and immediately silenced him by stating that Sydney was dead. I did not document any of this because I found her behavior extremely troubling. Then, Chad entered a fugue state from the shock and has not been able to remember anything about his life since. Is Chad Johnson even his real name? What is it that this woman doesn't want him to remember? What is Hollis Mazot doing to help her keep him an amnesiac? I don't even think this Sydney is really dead."

"Some of the girls were saying he was calling out for 'Cindy'."

"No. I distinctly heard Sydney."

"I've never heard that name for a woman before."

"I have. I can see how it could be mistaken for the much more familiar 'Cindy'."

"Thank you for sharing this, Verity. I've been racking my brain, trying to come up with a way to help poor Chad."

"We can work as a team, Libby. I'm sure there is something we can come up with if we put our heads together."

"I'm in. How much are you willing to risk to find the answers?"

"As much as necessary. Verity Ridgway never backs down from a challenge."

Chapter 9/ THE FINAL WEEK

Monday:

I am not ready to let go. I am not ready to abandon them. Not yet. Not now. But when I walk away from here on Friday, it will be forever. Perhaps, some day, I will be able to accept the cliché "It was not meant to be". The coldness of the finality descends upon me in the sun-filled staff lounge. You cannot expect to expose your unethical supervisors and hope for fair treatment from any remaining members of the profession. You cannot speak out for professional integrity and hope to coexist with its worst violators. How can you expect any trace of humanity behind their starched white exteriors? There was never any question that they would win in the end. How could there have been any hope of justice?

"Oh, I'm sorry – I didn't mean to disturb you." a delicate voice is behind me; in the doorway, I find Simone with a reticent smile.

"Simone – come in. I'm glad to see you."

"Are you sure? I didn't realize you were working in here."

"It wasn't important." I place the patients' charts on a side table, "I'm happy to see you. I would certainly enjoy your company."

"Thank you." she lingers in uncertainty.

"Please sit down." I urge her, touching her shoulder.

She complies silently, leaning forward on an uncomfortable chair.

"Everyone was smoking in the patients' lounge. I just wanted to breathe some clean air." she smiles distractedly, "It's so lonely here. I can't really get close to any of the others. I can't talk to them. And the staff – well..."

"I know it is difficult at times to relate to others in your environment. It can make you feel so alienated. Maybe you and I can have a little talk."

"They have to let me go home. My daughter needs me. She cannot study for her exams if I don't bake her favorite cookies. She always says she can't study without my cookies." Tears fill her eyes.

"It's okay. It's going to be okay." I place a hand over hers and she trembles.

"I should go." she rises suddenly; I watch this fragile woman fade into the corridor – alone and afraid.

"What's the story with that new guy, anyway?" Susan, one of my fellow trainees tosses her ponytail as she strolls in with our supervisor, Mrs. Clark.

"As I told all of you at conference this morning, I want all of you to stay away from Joe. He's only staying here until they can get him into the hospital in Newbridge. He ended up in this place because he followed a man he met in Ontario. The man wanted him off his back, so he had him committed here. But they don't want him; they are trying to get him into the other hospital, closer to his home town. I don't want to see any of you around him. Only male staff members can attempt therapy with him. He is terribly threatened by any member of the opposite sex. Only Rob can work with him until they can get rid of him."

I want to shake my head. In what century and under what rock is this woman living? What kind of a place is "Happy Valley"?

The group dissipates amidst snickers. I remain until all have vacated the lounge. Perhaps one can forgive Susan for her crass behavior, because of her youth, however, the mature trainees ten, twenty years my senior, are impossible to forgive. They whisper off-color jokes about the patients' predicaments on their way to the cafeteria for a cigarette fix.

"How are things for you, Marin?" Mrs. Clark catches a glimpse of me in my secluded corner, "How are you doing with Jason?"

"He's opening up to me more. I'm gaining insight into his situation."

"How is Simone?"

"Very pleasant and communicative. She seems so alone...I can't help wondering if she really belongs here. Couldn't she see her psychiatrist on an outpatient basis? She misses her family so much."

"Her husband and her doctor do not feel she is ready. Her husband had her committed, because she was getting very despondent – just sitting home and crying. Sometimes, she wouldn't even get dressed. He kept trying to think of activities to get her motivated – but she would not respond. She kept sinking deeper and deeper into a depression."

"Maybe she just needed his love. Maybe she needed to know somebody cared."

"It's not for us to say, Marin. Her husband and daughter do not want her back home. It upsets the girl to live in a climate of emotional strain."

"Isn't that selfish? Simone has needs, too. She's an intelligent, caring woman."

"You've got to maintain your objectivity, Marin. You don't really know Simone that well. She's a confused lady; she's very suspicious and manipulative."

Cold professionalism. Dedication only shuts doors in one's face. The only people who get ahead are the ones that play along with the system.

Tuesday:

"Now, Joanie, you know we cannot act like that here!" a stout, middle-aged attendant seizes a tomboyish girl, "Do you want to lose your privileges?"

"But he was cheating! He was cheating! Ask Debbie – she was there! She saw him! Nobody beats me at bumper pool if he's not cheating!"

"Joanie, now, calm down. Even if Billy were cheating, you cannot start hitting him."

"Let me go, Barb. I'm going to slash my wrists again! Nobody's going to stop me this time!" she storms out of the lounge with Barb behind her.

The other patients continue their card games in oblivion. The group now consists mostly of middle-aged men. The women seem to prefer the privacy of their claustrophobic rooms, except Sheila, tall, redheaded, and flamboyant, who sits with her legs crossed, smokes, and calls out sarcastic remarks to everyone within sight. She has a Master's Degree, and considers herself in the company of inferior beings.

Sitting beside me, Jason shrugs his shoulders with a smile of amusement. A few rays of the afternoon sun dance on his fair, scraggly hair falling over his boyish face.

"I don't understand why some people take everything so seriously. It's only a game. There are so many other things in life that really matter." he muses distractedly, "Maybe that is all Joanie has. That's why that game is so important to her."

His wisdom, so incongruous with his youth, is overwhelming. The patients' lounge, once again, becomes the center of activity.

"But I caught him eavesdropping! He was eavesdropping on Rob and Joe's conversation."

"All right, Joanie, that will be enough!" Barb chides her once again, "What did we just talk about in the hallway?"

"But I caught Abdul doing something wrong. He was listening to what you were saying to Joe, Rob." she nudges the attendant, "Aren't you going to punish him?"

"Whatever Abdul was doing is between him and us, Joanie. It does not concern you."

"You guys are all alike! I do you a favor and do you appreciate it? You bite my head off!" tears are streaming down the agitated girls' face. She removes her glasses and wipes them with her gingham shirt.

"They will get you with their magic!" Abdul shakes a finger at her, "You will never escape the magic! You think they can't find you here in this hospital – but they can find you no matter where you hide! They have the magic!"

"Drop dead, will you! You got me into trouble! If you hadn't been spying on Rob talking to the fruit, I wouldn't be in trouble now!"

As Jason leaves the ward for his appointment with his psychiatrist, I walk down the corridor to Simone's room. I find her with an afghan around her, curled up in one corner of her bed, rocking back and forth with a vacant stare.

"I never encouraged him. I never wanted it." she murmurs distractedly, "Dick blames me. But I did not want it."

"Who, Simone? Someone did something to hurt you. Can you tell me about it?" I place my hand over hers.

"He sent Dick out of town on business. He came to the house when I was alone."

"Who, Simone?"

"Dick never really believed me. He thought I lured him there. He said, the fact that I did not report it proved I wanted it, too. But, how could I report it? Dick's job...Ross would have fired him. Dick said I had a pathetic crush on Ross, and threw myself at him, but when he refused to enter into an affair with me, I accused him of rape...He believed him over me. He said I repulsed him. He wouldn't sleep in our room after that. He told the kids I was going through a nervous break-down. Then, he put me in here."

"Oh, Simone, that is so much pain for you to be carrying around alone, all this time." I hold her.

I long to protect her, comfort her, make this nightmare go away. I need to make things right for her.

"Simone has to have her medication now." a young, matter-of-fact staff nurse enters the room with a small plastic cup in one hand and a Dixie cup in the other. I keep an arm around Simone as she takes the sedatives out of the plastic cup obediently, and drinks the water out of the paper cup.

"Those pills are to make her rest." the nurse informs me coldly, "You have to leave her alone. She cannot get

95

proper rest if you are here. Come on, Simone, get under the covers." she draws the blinds efficiently.

"I'll be back later." I squeeze Simone's hand as we smile in mutual understanding.

She glances helplessly after me as the nurse ushers me out. Outside, Mrs. Clark is waiting in ambush.

"I want to talk to you."

I follow her wearily into the conference room.

"I'm taking you off Simone's case." she informs me, "You are getting too emotionally involved. You can no longer maintain your objectivity and you certainly cannot do much good for her like this. You have fostered a dependency in her, so she cannot function without you. Is that fair to her? What do you think will become of her once the rotation is over and you are gone? You make things pleasing and soft for her and do everything for her, so she never has to take the initiative for anything, and she can keep hiding in her shell. Is that the way you want her to remain? Don't you want her to learn to stand on her own feet?"

I do not dignify this diatribe with a response.

"And Jason – you have to start preparing him for your departure. Tomorrow, I am assigning you to Estelle. She is the most difficult and demanding patient on the ward and needs constant supervision and basic nursing care. She has Huntington's. She is deteriorating rapidly – both physically and emotionally. The rest of the patients feel uncomfortable around her, because of her uncontrollable muscle spasms and the constant twitching of her face. You'll have your hands full with her, so I won't assign another patient. As of right now, Simone and Jason are no longer your patients. They will be assigned to others, and you'll keep your contact to a minimum."

I can tell the sadistic bitch is enjoying every moment of this.

Wednesday:

Estelle is ostracized by all – staff and patients alike. They all look away uneasily. Barb cleans her up each time she vomits. She coaxes her to eat at lunchtime. Ken, the male nurse on staff, gives her medication and offers her words of encouragement. All others refuse to acknowledge her existence. An emaciated woman of forty with soft brown hair and enormous dark eyes, she is locked in private hell.

"They forget that she is human." Ken frowns, helping me scrub the remains of Estelle's breakfast from the linoleum.

"I'm sick! I'm sick! What's going to happen to me? Let me out of here! Let me get the hell out of here!" she is banging her fists on the table.

"Estelle, Estelle, let's go into the other room and sit down." I lead her away.

"I'm sick to my stomach! All the time. Sick to my stomach. They give me bad food. They give me bad medicine. They want to make me sick."

"No, Estelle, they don't want to make you sick."

"My hair is all itchy. I have lice."

"No, you don't have lice, but it's very warm in here. Maybe that's why you're itchy."

"No, I have lice!" she is desperately scratching her head, "I hate lice! My husband gave them to me! He was no good! He never bought me birth control pills. No good."

Her increased volume irritates several patients who begin vacating the lounge.

"My husband was no good. He gave me bugs. Bugs down there, too." she attempts to remove her undergarments, totally oblivious to the presence of the male patients, however, I prevent her from doing so.

Mrs. Clark enters the lounge and motions me to her side. Explaining to Estelle that I have to leave, I join my supervisor, and follow her through the locked door, down the narrow corridor, and into the tunnel that connects the two buildings.

"You are very good with Estelle." she praises me, "She doesn't get much attention. She must really appreciate the time you spend with her. She doesn't have anybody, except her two teenaged children, who beat her up and steal her welfare cheques."

All the other trainees are already settled in their seats around the bare mahogany table, eating chocolate bars. They snicker and whisper as I enter the room, while Mrs. Clark chats with a secretary outside the door.

After conference, I buy a cup of tea from the vending machine and sip it in a corner of the television room, the only lounge with a view. The warmth of the Styrofoam cup emanates a sense of security as I observe the traffic on the slushy road.

"You remind me of my pet cobra." Abdul is standing before me, "Rocky's my best friend. My mother's taking care of him for me. You look exactly like him."

"Thank you." I smile weakly, unexpectedly touched.

"You're welcome. You looked like you needed someone to cheer you up."

"You're very aware of people's moods, aren't you?"

"Yes. I know that a lot of people here have no hope. I also know Joanie is in danger. I keep warning her, but she doesn't listen. She's a very foolish girl. They are going to get her with their magic."

"Who are 'they', Abdul?"

"Those people on T.V. If you are not strong enough to resist, they get you with their magic. They watch you very closely. If you start to weaken, they come after you. Once you are theirs, you can never be free again."

Perhaps there's some logic to his reasoning, some concealed meaning. These tormented souls could teach so much to the rest of us.

"You know, what really matters is not how much money you've got, or how important your job is." I recall Jason's remarks from our walk on the grounds last week, "Some people have everything but they are not happy at all. All that matters is if you like what you're doing and you believe in yourself. You don't need anything else."

Thursday:

"Hello, Jenny."

Perplexed, I turn around to find Joe smiling into my eyes.

"Hello, Joe." I smile back, "My name is Marin, though."

"I'm sorry. You looked like a Jenny."

"Do I remind you of a Jenny you used to know?"

"No. I have never known a Jenny."

"If you prefer to call me Jenny, it's all right."

"Thank you. I was hoping I would get a chance to talk to you. You are the only one who ever smiles at me. Is it okay if I talk to you?"

"Of course." I motion him to sit at the table across from me, as I put down my charts.

"Everything is so awful." he bites his nails, "I can't stand it anymore."

"You are feeling a great deal of pain, aren't you?"

"It really hurts inside. I want to stop being gay and become straight, but I don't know how to do it."

"Joe, what matters is not whether you are straight or gay. What is important is being in a relationship where there is mutual love, respect, and nurturing."

"When I love someone, he never feels the same way. It is not just Todd. He was straight. Even gay men don't like me. I always feel so rejected. Maybe if I weren't gay, it would be different. I feel like a freak."

"Joe, you're not a freak. When someone who is good enough for you comes along, you will be loved and appreciated."

"People keep telling me I'm going to burn in hell."

"Caring about another human being and making a commitment is never wrong in God's eyes. It is who we are as people that matters, not our choice of partners. This is the 1980's. Attitudes are changing. But there will always be bigots. You need to be true to yourself and follow your own heart. The worst thing you could do would be to try to 'become straight', as you put it. Love yourself as you are."

"Thank you, Jenny. God bless you." tears fill his eyes as he leaves.

I gather my charts and return them to the nurses' station. No one appears to need me. I turn left toward the patients' rooms.

"Hi, it's me." I stand in the doorway.

"Marin, how nice to see you!" her eyes light up across the room.

"I wanted to see how you were. I don't like not being able to spend as much time with you."

"Oh, I understand. You have to do what your supervisor tells you."

"Rules can be so silly sometimes."

"Simone, your husband is here." a staff nurse appears behind us.

"Dick is here?" she is frozen, "He came to see me?"

"I'll give you some privacy." I start to leave, however, she clutches my hand.

"Please don't leave me."

A tall man in a business suit appears in the doorway and glances around him uneasily.

"Hi, Dick." she embraces him warmly, "It's so good to see you. I missed you so much." She kisses his cheek.

"Not here, Simone. Don't embarrass me." he pushes her away.

"I want you to meet the nice nurse who has been so kind to me. Her name is Marin."

"How do you do." he shakes my hand.

"Pleased to meet you."

"How have you been, Simone?" he asks coldly, "You look well."

"I'm fine, Dick. I'm doing really well. Everybody says so. I'm well enough to come home now and take care of you and Stephanie."

"It's a bit premature for that."

"How is my little girl? Is she all right?"

"We're both managing just fine." he cuts her off.

"I miss her, Dick. I never see her."

"You certainly cannot expect me to bring her to...to this place!" he retorts, "You cannot be so selfish as to expose her to such a frightening environment."

"I'm sorry." she murmurs softly.

"Well, I must be going now." he starts toward the door, "I'm very pleased with your progress."

"When will I ever see you again, Dick?"

"I can't say for certain. I expect to be tied up with meetings for quite a while."

"Dick – "she pleads weakly, "Please get me out of here. Please. I'm so drugged, I cannot think straight."

"It's not up to me, Simone. You have to get better before I can take you home. Those drugs are for your own good. If you can't even accept that, you're a long way from being well."

"I'm over-sedated all the time. It numbs all my emotions. I don't want to feel this way. I want to be myself, feel my natural emotions. I don't need all these drugs. I'm so much stronger now."

"I'm pleased that you feel better, but I don't think you're ready to resume your old life. You have to do what Dr. Dietrich tells you, and take all your pills."

"Would you like to see the painting I did?" she smiles suddenly.

"No, I don't have time right now."

"But it's a painting of our cottage in autumn. It's surrounded by beautiful foliage."

"I'm sure it's lovely, dear. I'll see it next time. I have to go now." kissing her forehead, he disappears without another glance.

Friday:

Entering the conference room, I am met with a peculiar hush and an unusual look of solicitude on Mrs. Clark's face.

"I want you girls to go on duty now. There is no conference this morning. Marin, you stay. I would like to speak with you."

Something is not right. What have I done now? What dreadful deed have I committed that I cannot even be humiliated before my colleagues?

"Sit down, Marin." she is unusually kind, "There is something you have to know."

"Mrs. Clark, did I do something disastrous?"

"No, no. Nothing like that."

The silence hangs in icicles between us. She stands up, walks over to the window overlooking the pulp and paper mill, her back turned to me.

"There's no easy way to tell you this, Marin."

"No. It's not...It can't be..." I cannot bring myself to utter the words, for doing so may confirm it.

She nods knowingly.

"No. No." I shake my head, "It's not true."

"It is true. I'm sorry."

"No. I don't believe you." I expect to awaken any minute to discover that this is a nightmare, however, it does not happen.

"They found her at four o'clock this morning when they went in to give her morning meds. She had hanged herself with the scarf her husband had given her on her birthday. She did not leave a note. On her night table, she had placed an old photograph of her family...Marin...Where are you going?"

Chapter 10/ ONE AND ONLY

"My Sweet Jack," Sydney wrote in her black leather-bound journal with a green felt-tip marker, "I'm writing this journal entry because in the event that you might return home some day and I am no longer among the living, hopefully, you will read this and understand why I had to do the things I did."

She paused to dab at her eyes with a tissue from the floral cardboard dispenser beside her. She was sprawled across her bed on the white duvet cover. Nancy Wilson's caressing rendition of "My One And Only Love" softened the sound of the howling wind outside.

"Jack, I have never loved anyone the way I love you – and I know I never will." she wrote, "We had so much love; we could've been so happy...but the life we were building was stolen from us. We had so little time together. The pain of losing you is something I can never come to terms with, Jack. I do not want to continue my meaningless existence like this. When I believed you were dead, all I could think about was joining you. Now that it's been revealed your stepmother faked your death to get you away from me, I realize I need to release you. I cannot stop wondering: Did I give up too quickly, my love? Did I let you go too easily? Perhaps, I should have fought harder for you, for us...But I have no strength left in me to remain in limbo like this. For reasons I may never learn, you have chosen to remain in hiding. You've obviously decided to cut me out of your life. Why didn't you fight for me, Jack? Why didn't you fight for us? Why did you acquiesce to Audrey's demands? Tony and

Warren are leaving no stone unturned. Should they find you, will you still choose to keep me out of your life? Wherever you are, Jack, whoever you are with, I hope you are happy, safe, and loved. That is what I want for you. I am always going to love you, Jack. That is why I am now releasing you. Good-bye, my love."

By now, Nancy Wilson had grown silent. Sydney closed her journal, repositioned herself on the bed and placed her head on the pillow. The tears came in a torrent as nightfall engulfed her.

* * *

In the cold hush of Waterloo Row, they walked hand in hand under the dark sky.

"So, your uncle is amping up the search tactics. You sure have an interesting family, Doe." he squeezed her hand.

"I wish I didn't, J.T." she had started calling him J.T. for John Thomas, instead of Jack.

"I'm glad you're not like the rest of them."

"Warren is initially being discreet about the search, so Aunt Audrey wouldn't get skittish and take off with Jack to a new location. But he couldn't get any leads. It seemed she was always ten steps ahead of his detectives. I know it sounds paranoid, but you'd almost think someone here was keeping tabs on the detectives and deliberately leading them astray."

"It's not paranoid at all. Actually, that is quite feasible. She must have someone helping her on this end. She obviously has connections, since she initially pulled off the body switch. We're investigating the medical staff who were present when Jack was pronounced dead. We're closing in on whoever is behind this."

"Thank God for the witness who came forward to say he saw Billy, the homeless man being approached by those men in the alley behind the soup kitchen and then being led away by them into a dark van on the night Jack was pronounced dead. The man on the gurney Tony and I saw in the hospital elevator who was all bandaged up getting airlifted that night was actually Jack. That night was the last time anyone saw Billy. Aunt Audrey demanded the body be cremated immediately."

"She cooked up quite a scheme."

"What I don't understand is: Why didn't Jack try to escape and return to Sydney? I know he's madly in love with her. He'd never willingly stay away from her."

"Something is preventing him from coming home. He is most likely being held captive against his will."

"Warren's going at this with all guns blazing now. All the media outlets in Canada and U.S. have the real dirt."

"Let the chips fall where they may. No matter how you go about it, people are going to be hurt, Doe."

"I don't know if Sydney can survive this, J.T. She's been in a very deep depression for over a year and she might never recover."

* * *

"This story's just in: International recording star Jack Chandler, whose death was reported last year, has been discovered to be living and is officially a missing person. He might be living under a different identity, and is likely to be with Audrey Chandler, his stepmother, who is suspected of abducting him. If you see either one of them, please contact your local police department.

Jack Chandler owned "Chandler's Lounge" in Beavertown, New Brunswick, Canada, which was destroyed last January in a spectacular blaze. He is married to Sydney Goldstein, the daughter of a well-respected businessman in that community. Audrey Chandler is from the prominent Horncastle family of Beavertown.

We'll keep you informed of all new developments."

Ribby picked up the receiver promptly and whispered:

"Hello...Oh, Cece...I'm whispering because Chad's asleep in the other room...Yes, I watched the news, too...We need to call the police. We have an obligation to report this, now that we know who he is and where he belongs. He's almost completely weaned off the drugs now. It's good to know we did the right thing and got him away from his stepmother...I'll make the call right now..."

Chapter 11/ ON THE MOVE

He kept his head lowered during the Greyhound ride and avoided eye contact with the white-haired woman beside him. He could not blame Ribby and Cece for blowing the whistle on him. The snippets of their phone conversation he had overheard from his bedroom had allowed him to piece together some of the facts: The police were looking for him and his mother, who, apparently was his stepmother. She had helped him escape, to evade the authorities. He must have committed a crime – or multiple crimes, if she felt a need to change their names and go into hiding. He wondered what his misdeeds were: Burglary? Armed robbery? Assault? Murder? He hoped he was not a murderer. He would not be able to live with himself then. The newscasts did not reveal any background on what he had done and why it had been necessary to go into hiding. It might be that he was not a criminal himself but in danger from criminals, for reasons he could not begin to imagine. With his face plastered on T.V. screens across the country, and in Canada, he needed to alter his physical appearance. One factor working in his favor was that, during his weeks at the cottage weaning off Dr. Mazot's deadly cocktail, he had allowed himself to adopt the appearance of a rugged mountain man, unlike the well-dressed, clean-shaven blond man in the photos being circulated by the media. He had a bushy beard now, and long scraggly hair reaching his shoulders. It was no longer blond – but a muddy brown. All he needed now was a pair of amber-tinted glasses to conceal his facial features. The clothing left behind in the closet of his room at the cottage had been a blessing: Plaid flannel shirts, work pants, warm quilted jackets, parkas, snow boots. A pang of guilt tugged at him for his thievery, however, there had not been an alternate solution available at the time. He barely had time to pack the contents of the closet into the suitcase and two duffle bags he had found, and climb out of the window before the authorities could arrest him. He had emptied out the joint bank account he had with his mother before leaving for the cabin, anticipating an adventure-filled road trip with Cicely and Ribby across Canada. Instead, he was a fugitive from justice.

Tears filled his eyes. This time, he was all alone in the world. He needed to find a city where no one could track him down. A place where he could become lost in the crowd. Just another face without a name. Just another displaced soul.

* * *

"We were so damn close!" Warren banged his fist on the red chrome table in the diner.

"According to the retired nurse who reported it, he had been in Boston the entire time." J.T. said.

"Fuck! And our guys kept getting fed false leads by that son of a bitch brother of mine!"

"But why did he take off like that?" Dottie said.

"The nurse said he's in a fugue state and doesn't remember anything. He must've been frightened when he overheard her talking about calling the police about him." J.T. said.

"Audrey flew the coop, of course, as soon as the news hit the fan." Warren shook his head, "She probably has guys looking for him, too. Let's just hope either our guys or the authorities find him before her goons do."

"Jack doesn't have anyone looking out for him now." Dottie said, "Sounds like the nurses were making sure he was okay before. Now, he's all alone, who knows where, and he must be terrified."

* * *

And now, this was his life. For how long, he did not know. Washing dishes at a dilapidated, and filthy restaurant in the bowels of New York City. He did not interact with the customers. They were a motley crew of winos, junkies and disheveled older men down on their luck, no doubt with a tragic story, still carrying the wounds from the past, searching for a one-way ticket to Oblivion. He avoided friendly banter with the other fellows who worked there, kept the conversation limited to small talk. He asked no personal questions and gave them no leeway to ask him anything intrusive. He even created a cover story: He needed to get home after work to take care of his cancer-stricken girlfriend. He also told them the only time he ventured out of their apartment was to run errands.

They were pleasant enough fellows and they accepted him. He could not ask for any better. Lou, the other dish-washer was a down-on-his-luck guy who kept to himself. Mike the cook, and Al the cleaner were middle-aged family men. Norm the young delivery guy with the ponytail somehow made him nervous. They, undoubtedly, all had their stories. Perhaps they knew about each other's but did not discuss them in his presence.

Mike was singing "O Sole Mio" in Italian as he prepared spaghetti and meatballs.

"Your talent's being wasted here, honey. Why don't you audition for a part in a Broadway musical?" Rosie, the aging server brought more dirty dishes into the kitchen, "These are the absolute last. All the customers cleared out."

Her hair was dyed black and fastened in a bun at the nape of her neck. Turquoise eyeshadow framed her weary hazel eyes. Dark pencil lines covered her sparse eyebrows. Her lipstick was a garish shade of red.

"I've got mouths to feed, Rosie." Mike shot back.

"Hey kids, what do you say we form our own musical group?" Rosie beamed, "Mike here can sing. I can be the back-up singer. Ed, you play the drums. Lou, you play the guitar. What do you say, kids?"

"I'm in." Lou said.

"Sure you are. You've got no family responsibilities." Mike said.

"I'm in, too." Ed said, "Can't say no to one night a week to myself."

"Don't look at me." Mike stated emphatically.

"Come on, Mike. It'll be fun."

"I got no time."

"What about you, Harry?" Rosie called out.

Receiving no response, she glanced quizzically at the others.

"Hey, pal! The lady asked you a question!" Mike called out.

Jack bolted. Unaccustomed to yet another false identity, he did not always respond promptly.

"I'm sorry. Didn't hear you. Must've been daydreaming." he stammered.

"That's okay, Harry." Rosie reassured him, "We're going to start a music group. Ed plays the drums; Lou plays the guitar. I can be the back-up singer. But Mike refuses to be our singer."

"Got no time for that stuff." Mike said.

"What talent do you have, Harry?" Ed asked.

"I'm afraid I don't have any. I'm tone deaf."

"That's too bad. Maybe you can do some publicity for us, then."

"I'm no good at that sort of thing, either, Rosie."

"Everybody's good at something. You must have something to contribute." Ed said.

"Not me. I'm afraid I'm not much good at anything, fellas."

"He has to take care of his lady." Mike reminded them, "Leave the poor guy alone. He's got his hands full."

"It was only a pipe dream. It would never have worked, anyway." Rosie sighed, "Who's going to pay money to hear us?"

"Speaking of singing, any of you heard anything new about that missing singer?" Mike asked.

"Disappeared into thin air. No sightings anywhere." Rosie said, "His poor wife's still begging him to come home on the news."

"She's his sixth wife." Ed flashed a toothless grin; his cheeks were sunken and his skin weather-beaten like old leather upholstery.

"He sure got around." Mike laughed.

"That's not all." Rosie said, "He had an ex-fiancée who was murdered just before he disappeared. The murder was never solved. Both his club and the dead woman's apartment were torched."

Jack submerged his trembling hands in the sudsy water. Six wives and an ex-fiancée who was murdered? Two arson fires? What kind of a monster was he? He did not deserve to live. His wife needed to forget about him and move on. All of the people looking for him and begging him to return would be better off without the likes of him.

"Here's the most likely scenario: He cheated on the ex-fiancée with the one he later married." Rosie mused, "Maybe he killed off the jilted woman when she made a fuss. He doesn't sound like a nice person at all. Not someone I'd like to meet, for sure."

"All celebrities are like that." Ed said, "Can't be loyal to anyone."

"No wonder he hasn't gone back home." Mike said.

"All that amnesia stuff's probably fake." Lou said, "He's on the run."

"Rich, spoiled Mama's Boy." Mike shook his head in disdain, turning off the gas burner, "Tomorrow's spaghetti and meatballs special's ready."

"You can go home now, Mike. I can freeze the food before Moe and I close up." Rosie said.

"Thanks, Rosie." he removed his apron and hung it on the rack, "See you folks tomorrow. Need a lift, Harry?"

Flushed and flustered, Jack managed to mumble.

"No thanks, Mike. I'll be fine."

"How 'bout you, Ed?"

"Gee, thanks, Mike."

Lou had a ride with Mike on a regular basis and he followed the two of them quietly. Jack waited for the other men to leave before starting home.

"You all right, son?" Rosie smiled solicitously.

"Everything's fine, Rosie. See you tomorrow." he waved on his way out.

This was his life now, working at Moe's dive and walking home to his cage hotel on Skid Row. He started the lonely walk back to "The White House Hotel", his humble refuge from the world, the single room occupancy hotel with cubicles accommodating nothing more than narrow cots. This was his home. The home he shared with other broken men.

He walked briskly through the dark streets, keeping his eyes averted from people. Then, that sweet voice he heard in his dreams every night whispered in his ear: "I'm always going to love you, Jack."

He wearily opened the door to his building, walked past the front desk where Stu was snoring, ascended the creaky stairs to the narrow second floor hallway. Pete, the World War I veteran had his door open. He was seated on his cot, reading an ancient hard-cover book. He glanced up at him and greeted him congenially.

"Hi, Harry."

"Hi, Pete. How's it going?"

"Can't complain. How about you?"

115

"Me, too, Pete. Me, too."

He lay on his cot, feeling every spring digging into his back, and glanced up at the low lattice-work ceiling he almost hit his head on every night. This was where he belonged, in this derelict flophouse with all the other dispossessed souls, waiting for death.

Chapter 12/ UPHOLDING HIGH MORALS

In the cold hush of Waterloo Row, they walked hand in hand. The firm grip of his big hand felt warm and reassuring. He had been remarkably patient with her. It would not be fair to expect him to wait any longer. She paused at the corner of Shore Street and gazed up at him.

"Don't take me home."

"Why not? Where do you want to go?" he asked.

"To your apartment."

"Why? Do you want to avoid someone at your house? Are your parents still giving you a hard time about your low GPA?"

"No. Nothing like that." she laughed softly, "They've given up on me."

"I'm glad they're not nagging you about that anymore."

"They said, as long as I don't fail, they're okay with it, because they have very low expectations of me by now."

"Don't pay any attention to them." he squeezed her hand and led her toward the pristine mid-century building.

The unspoken loomed between them. Neither dared utter a word about it.

J.T. opened the security door with his key. A frail, elderly man in a stained white singlet greeted them in the lobby, grey chest hairs sprouting wildly above the threadbare undergarment.

"No funny business, sonny." he shook a nicotine-stained finger at J.T.

"Don't worry, Ralph." he smiled.

"I run a clean building, you know. I don't put up with partyin' an' carousin'. Can't bring women up unless you're married. Better behave yourselves."

"We're engaged." J.T. said, "And, don't worry: No funny business."

"We had all kinds of complaints from the other tenants when that singer and his floozy were shacked up here. She was bringing all sorts of men up to the apartment when he wasn't around. The other tenants didn't feel safe with strangers wandering around the hallways."

Dottie and J.T. met each other's gaze uncomfortably.

"Now, we're real strict about who's comin' an' goin' around here."

"I don't blame you, Ralph. You can't be too careful these days." J.T. said, winking at Dottie.

"Heard that singer feller went missin' an' his floozy got herself murdered. Good thing it happened after they left here. Don't want their sort around here again."

"Don't worry, Ralph."

"Actually," Dottie said, "I should go home. I can borrow that Billy Joel album another time. I need to study for my exams, anyway." she started back toward the security door.

"I'll walk you home. See you later, Ralph." J.T. followed her.

"Don't' let him get to you." he said, aware of her retreating into herself.

"J.T., why don't we elope?" she spoke suddenly.

"Elope? Honey, what brought this on?"

"It would be straightforward and uncomplicated. No pomp and circumstance. Just us and a couple of witnesses. You could get one of your buddies and I'll get Peggy. We'll go to City Hall and get it done. Are you on board with this idea, J.T.?"

"Sounds good to me, but your family's going to be upset."

"The members who actually matter won't be. What about your family?"

"They're intimidated by the idea of being in the same room as your legendary family. This would be a great relief for them."

"Then, let's do it."

"What brought this on, Doe?"

"I was thinking about the fact that I haven't been fair to you."

"How?"

"Expecting you to wait forever."

"I understand your reasons for being afraid. What your uncle did to you was reprehensible."

"You're a saint."

"I'm no saint. You should never have had to go through that."

"Thank you."

"If we had a traditional wedding, I'd have a hard time controlling myself and probably kill the bastard or put him in the hospital for a long time."

"Let's elope right away."

"How about next month after your graduation?"

"Sounds perfect."

He kissed her softly on the forehead and enclosed her small hand in his large one. They walked slowly in the falling dusk.

* * *

"I want her out of here before July. Cousin Muriel's coming to visit from Nova Scotia and I don't want her to know about your shameful little indiscretion." Mildred stood in the doorway of Tony' suite.

"Where is she going to go?"

"That's your concern, not mine. I just want her gone. Rent her an apartment; put her up in a hotel; I don't really care."

"You're all heart, Mother." he picked up his briefcase and started toward the stairs.

"She's got herself ensconced in Audrey's old suite, being waited on hand and foot. Once the baby's born and she gets accustomed to taking care of it, there's no need for her to be taking up space here anymore. I want to use that as a guest suite." she followed behind him on the stairs.

"I'll take care of it."

"See that you do, dear."

"I'm not surprised Alexandra broke things off with you when she got wind of your debauchery."

"Good-bye, Mother." he slammed the front door behind him.

Mildred began wailing; soon, she was able to attract the attention she craved.

"What is it, Mil, dear?" Annette appeared around the corner.

"This younger generation's so impertinent." she sobbed.

"What did Tony do this time?"

"I asked him very politely to find other accommodations for his...his...whatever you want to call her, and he bit my head off."

"Don't let him get to you, dear." Annette hugged her.

"You and I have so much trouble with our children, Annette, dear; don't we?"

"We certainly do."

"At least, we have each other to turn to."

"And, Maxine's scrumptious muffins. Let's go get some now." Annette led her away.

Chapter 13/ FAMILIAR FACE

She walked out into the crisp night air and the scent of moist earth. Her bones ached from the damp spring mornings, but she was too keyed up to dwell on it. Lea and baby were sleeping peacefully, totally exhausted following thirteen hours of labor. She and Lea had shared an exhilarating experience and forged a unique bond. Her godchild, Aurelie Brette Horncastle had come into the world at seven pounds, ten ounces, pink and soft, trusting and good. She prayed no one would steal her innocence too young. She prayed Aurelie would be surrounded with love and guidance, not left to her own devices to find her way in the world. She prayed well-meaning but misguided adults would not let her down – would not suffocate her with clichéd advice and undermine her instincts.

In two months, Keir would graduate from high school and move into the garage apartment of Josh's house. In September, he would begin studying Computer Science. Her older son was leaving the nest; soon, it would be just her and Toby for another two years until he joined his brother.

The streets were silent. Only twelve more blocks, she reminded herself. This long walk would clear her head. She would not drink tonight. She would allow herself to feel every emotion, every gut-wrenching emotion she had denied all these years. She longed to experience life without the alcoholic haze that had become her permanent state of mind. She was not like her father. No, she would never be a hopeless drunk like him.

She found Tony on her front porch with a box of Minnie's minibites.

"Don't tell me you walked!" he said in astonishment, "I expected to see a cab pull up."

"It was much too nice out to be in a stuffy taxi."

"There are a lot of crazy dopeheads out on the streets. It's not safe for you to be walking alone at this hour."

"Don't worry, sweetheart. I can take care of myself. I didn't expect to see you here."

"After you called from the hospital to tell me about the birth of my daughter, I had to come and talk to you."

"Come on in." she reached in her pocketbook for her keys and opened the door.

"I'm going up there first thing in the morning." he said, "I can't believe it: I have a daughter!"

"Lea and the baby can move in here with me into Keir's room in July now that he's going to be a big man on the campus."

"I'll buy the crib and the baby supplies. I don't think Mother'll let her keep my old crib. We'll furnish the room before she and the baby arrive. Can you come shopping with me? I wouldn't know what to look for."

"Sure, hon. No doubt we'll provide fodder for delicious gossip around town." she winked.

"I can hire a couple of guys to clean and paint the room first."

"A soft blush pink with fresh sprout green accents would be bright and cheerful."

"I'll talk to your landlord, so he doesn't get hot under the collar. Have you and Lea talked about her living here?"

"No. We didn't realize Keir was going to move out."

"This is extremely magnanimous of you, Brett. You never cease to amaze me."

She smiled weakly.

"Let's have a drink to celebrate." he said brightly, "I bought a bottle of champagne for this occasion. I'll go out to the car and get it."

"I don't think I'll have any. You go ahead. I'll keep you company, but I'll stick with my club soda."

"Brett, what is this about?"

"Being instrumental in bringing new life into the world is a sobering experience. It makes me want to try harder to be a better person, to try to make up for the way I've been living all these years."

"There's nothing wrong with the way you've been living." he came up behind her and encircled her waist with his arms, "You are the most beautiful, most exciting woman I've ever known. You are the only woman I have ever loved."

"I love you, too, sweetheart. But you know I'm not good for you...I'm not good for anyone."

"You are the only good thing that has ever happened to me." he attempted to kiss her, but was gently pushed away, "Chuck says Ron Mitton's history. Brett, tell me you can't get me out of your system, either. We are bound together. We're soulmates. Nothing can diminish our love for one another. No matter how much we deny it, how hard we try to stay away from each other, we can't deny it."

"I can't be with anyone, sweetheart. I need to sort through things, do some soul searching." she said, "It's long overdue. In July, I'll be fifty-four years old. I can't rely on booze and sex to make me feel alive anymore. I need to look long and hard in the mirror and learn to like the person I see. And, I can't do that if I allow myself to be emotionally dependent on anyone. I have to stand back and look at myself objectively. I can only do that if I'm alone."

"You don't need to be alone. I can hold your hand while you do your soul searching."

"Sweetheart, if you are here to make life soft and comfortable for me, I cannot grow. I need to learn to feel all the pain I've stuffed in, all the pain I've been medicating away with booze and sex to keep myself from feeling it. I need to face my demons alone."

"What brought all this on? It's not just Lea and the baby, is it?"

She did not respond. She had not heard him.

"Brett, what is it?"

She had forgotten Tony was with her.

"Don't shut me out." he pulled her into an embrace.

She put up no resistance. Limp as a rag doll, she nestled in his arms and sobbed.

* * *

"I wish I could see 'Cats'." Rosie sighed.

"If you want to see cats, just go out in the back alley." Mike snapped back.

"See what I've got to live with?" Rosie turned to Jack.

125

"What the hell is this 'Cats', anyway?" Mike said, "A new group?"

"It's a musical making its world debut in London. When it comes to Broadway, I want to see it."

"In your dreams."

"You've got to become more cultured, Mike."

"There's nothing wrong with my culture. I pay my bills and keep a roof over my family's head. Culture don't pay the rent, Rosie. Broadway stars: They're nothing but a flash in the pan. Wouldn't want none of my kids going that route."

Jack could see Rosie cringing inwardly at Mike's grammar.

"Don't squash their dreams if that's what they want to pursue, Mike." Rosie said.

"Dreams don't put food on the table. They need a steady job. They don't need that highbrow stuff."

"You're incorrigible, Mike." Rosie shook her head.

"Don't be getting too big for your britches now, Rosie. You're no Ethel Merman. You're just one of us."

"Nothing wrong with culture, Mike. You tell him, Harry. You look like a cultured guy."

"Me?" Jack said in astonishment, "I'm just a drifter working at odd jobs here and there."

"Well, you've got an air of sophistication about you, honey."

"I wouldn't know about that."

"Two cheeseburger platters." Matt, the new young server burst in through the swinging door.

Jack wished he could see "Cats" himself. He was getting tired of life as a fugitive. He needed to put down roots, have someone to call his own. He missed Cicely and their carefree but brief time together. They could have had a future. She must have moved on by now and found someone else. Tears escaped from his eyes and he discreetly wiped them with his sleeve. He was all alone in the world.

"Got the sniffles, honey?" Rosie said, "I always get sick in the spring, too."

"I'm okay."

"Why don't you go home early, Harry? You don't look so good. I can help Lou with the dishes now that we've got Matt helping me serve tables."

"Thanks, Rosie."

"You go home and rest, dear. See you tomorrow."

On his way out, he heard Mike saying "You're sweet on that boy, Rosie."

"Cut it out, Mike. He's a lost soul. He needs someone to look out for him."

He took a circuitous route to take advantage of the warm spring air, and found himself humming "My One And Only Love". That face from his dreams appeared before him again: Sydney. He wished he could remember her better. What a beautiful face, shy smile, and those sad eyes like a wounded fawn. And such an unusual name – an aristocratic name. That song always reminded him of her and filled him with an inexplicable sense of longing.

He allowed his feet to take him where they longed. Crowds were gathering in shimmering attire at the Theater District.

"Give that poor man a quarter, Arthur." a woman in a sable coat nudged her male companion.

"Yes, dear." he sighed and reluctantly reached in his pocket for loose change.

The woman had a stern face marked with deep wrinkles further emphasized by heavy pancake make-up. Her glossy black hair was in a severe bun at the nape of her neck. The man approached him tentatively.

"Here you go, old chap."

"No thank you." Jack said promptly.

"Take it. You look like you could use it."

"I'm all right." he protested, turning crimson.

"Suit yourself, then." he returned to the woman's side.

Not far from him, a group of men in trendy attire were observing this interaction. Humiliated by the attention he had attracted, he attempted to walk away, only to hear a voice behind him.

"Jack! Jack Chandler! As I live and breathe! It's you, isn't it?"

Jack quickened his steps.

"Jack, it's me! Stephen." the man continued to follow him.

"I'm afraid you're confusing me with someone else, sir." he said softly without turning around.

"No, I'm not. I'd know you anywhere. Even in this ridiculous getup, Jack."

"You're mistaken. I'm not Jack. My name's Harry Adams."

"You don't have to pretend around me, Jack. I know it's you. Don't be afraid. Turn around."

"Please, just go away."

"Jack, do you realize everyone's been looking for you?"

"Look, I don't want any trouble. Please just walk away and tell your friends it was a case of mistaken identity." he turned around to face the handsome stranger.

"But why, Jack? Why don't you want to be found?"

"Why do you think?"

"I honestly haven't got a clue." he laughed softly.

"You can't tell anyone you saw me here tonight."

"I don't understand. Who are you running from, Jack?"

"The police."

"Why? What have you done?"

"It's all over the news. They're looking for me. I killed someone named Linda, torched my own business, faked my own death by killing an innocent man."

"Jack do you remember anything at all yet?"

"I can't remember anything. All I know is what I heard on the news. One scandal after another. I stopped listening after a while."

"Hold on a second. You did not kill Linda."

"How do you know? Her murder's never been solved."

"No one suspects you. She was killed when you were in Intensive Care. The person they suspect is her accomplice, who torched your club under her instructions. You haven't done anything wrong."

"How do you know all this?"

"It's all over the news. As for faking your death, you had nothing to do with that, either. Your stepmother orchestrated everything to get you away from your gold-digging wife."

"Sydney?"

"Yes. She had to get you away from her before she bled you dry."

"I can't believe that."

"It's true. I still have contacts in Beavertown who keep me up to date on these details. She lured you away from Linda."

"I can't remember any of it. The doctor in Boston did some bizarre experiments on me. He hypnotized me and drugged me."

"It's all in the past now. That doctor and your stepmother are both wanted by the authorities, both here and in Canada."

"You mean I've been hiding out for no good reason?"

"That's exactly what I've been trying to tell you."

"Then, I need to go back. All those people are worried about me. They have a right to know."

"You can't! You can't let Sydney get her hooks into you again! You need time to sort things through in your mind."

"I can't let all those people keep worrying."

"Why don't you stay with me while you get your head together? You can fortify yourself for a while. Then, you can go back more rested and ready to face all those people."

"I don't want to be an imposition. It wouldn't be right. I can't even remember you, Stephen. You seem like a very nice fellow, but I feel like I've just met you. How do we know each other?"

"I worked for you, Jack. I was a singer at your club, Chandler's Lounge. We were friends...good friends...more than friends."

"You mean we...?"

"Yes."

"What happened to make us part ways?"

"Beavertown was a stifling, homophobic, stagnant small town. I needed to get away, but you chose to remain with your family. We parted amicably, of course. There were no hard feelings on either side."

"This is an awful lot of information to process."

It had not occurred to him that he might have been bisexual. He was an enigma to himself.

"You can take all the time you need to process it. Come and stay at my place. Don't worry: No strings attached. We can go pick up your stuff from your place tonight. Where are you living?"

"The White House Hotel."

"Sylvia's hotel."

"Sylvia's hotel? I don't understand."

"The president of the company that owns the building is a woman named Sylvia."

Sylvia. Why was that name so familiar? Was it familiar to Stephen, as well? Why else would he have mentioned it?

"Does she have more than one hotel?"

"Not sure. Why?"

"I don't know. There's something familiar about 'Sylvia's hotel'."

"You must be thinking about the Sylvia Hotel in Vancouver, Canada. You stayed there when you were on tour."

"Vancouver. Did I ever live there?"

"I don't think so."

"I feel there's something special about the name Sylvia."

"It was your mother's name."

"My mother?"

"She died when you were young. Your dad later married Audrey Horncastle."

"It makes sense now. Thank you for filling in the blanks for me, Stephen."

"You're welcome. Why don't you come and meet my friends?"

"Looking like this?"

"Tell you what: I'll go over and tell them to go ahead to see the play and go on to the restaurant where we reserved a table for four. I'll say that I'll be joining them later with a friend. Then, you and I can go to my place and get you all cleaned up, looking like yourself again."

"Thank you, Stephen. I'll get a better paying job and pay you back."

"Don't worry about that. Where are you working now?"

"I'm washing dishes at a greasy spoon."

"No more of that. You can get a gig at a club. I know most of the owners. You can use a stage name if you like."

"Do you still sing?"

"No. I'm in advertising now. Do you want to wait here while I go and talk to Kent and Aydin?"

"Sure."

"Promise you won't take off?"

"Scout's Honor. You missed the play because of me."

"Don't worry. From what I've heard about this play, I'm not missing much. It's a silly, juvenile comedy. We had free tickets from Kent's brother-in-law. That's the only reason we decided to see it. Come on: I don't live far from here. I'll be right back."

As he watched Stephen run back toward the lively crowd, a warmth rose inside him. Things were going to work out, after all.

Chapter 14/ LIFTED VEIL

Hushed voices in the garden tugged playfully at the fringes of her consciousness. She pulled up her duvet over her ears and returned to sleep.

"She's going to find out sooner or later." Eli whispered, standing under the silver maple with Aunt Ethel, "Hiding her newspaper will only delay the inevitable."

"Better later than sooner." Ethel persisted.

"What if she hears about it on the radio or T.V., on the subway, at the lunch counter, or at the shop from a customer? People love to gossip. Isn't it better for her to find out in a more tactful way from one of us, so she can process it?"

"I have to admit, you're right, Eli."

"We can't put it off. Why don't you and Ira give her the day off and let me speak to her? Let me be the one to break it to her."

"You're such a good friend to her, Eli." she handed him the newspaper in her hand.

"I'll tell her the shop's closed today due to a burst pipe."

"Thank you, Eli." she patted his shoulder.

Eli returned to the coach house, climbed the stairs softly, and returned to his apartment. He placed the newspaper on top of his and took them to his bedroom to keep them temporarily out of sight. His eyes lingered on the front page photograph. He sighed. A smiling Jack Chandler was seated at a table beside another handsome man. Their hands were linked. The caption beneath read:

"The elusive jazz singer Jack Chandler has been spotted at last, happily reunited with his long-lost love interest, Stephen Browne. The pair is enjoying a romantic evening of dinner and dancing at 'Limelight'."

Eli recognized the place, a posh establishment in New York known for its elite gay clientele. He returned to the kitchen, and began preparations for breakfast for two in agonizing silence. He beat the eggs, unleashing his rage on the delicate crepe batter. That spoiled mama's boy must have regained his memory, if he remembered this Stephen fellow, and he must have chosen to be with him in New York instead of returning home to his wife.

He arranged the crepes on two plates, rolled with a strawberry and clotted cream filling and a drizzle of chocolate sauce on top. He poured freshly brewed coffee into two blue and white artisan mugs, folded the cloth napkins into fan shapes, and poured pineapple juice into grey tinted glasses.

He tiptoed down the hall to her door and knocked. There was no response.

"Sydney?" he called out.

"Just a second, Eli." he heard her from the bedroom; her footsteps came nearer and she opened the door.

"Hi. What's up?" she asked groggily, her dark unruly curls framing her face.

"I have breakfast ready. You have no work today. There's a plumbing issue at the shop and it's closed, so, just come as you are."

"Like this?" she glanced down at her battered robe wrapped around her tightly.

"What's wrong with that?"

"My hair's a mess."

"That's the latest style."

"Okay, then, but I hope you didn't go to too much trouble." she followed him to his apartment.

"No trouble at all."

"Liar." she winked, "I really wish you hadn't."

"I told you, no trouble. I enjoy doing this sort of thing. Don't deny me this small pleasure."

"Thank you, Eli." she smiled brightly, "This is very nice of you."

She did not catch his wistful glances in her direction as she savored his creation and engaged in lighthearted conversation.

As they moved to the living room, she glanced around her quizzically.

"No newspaper today? I didn't see one outside my door and it looks like you didn't get one, either."

"Sydney, about that...Please sit down." he motioned to the sofa. "We need to talk, Syd."

"You're scaring me. Is it something about my parents?"

"No. They're fine."

"Someone else from back home?"

"Everybody's fine; don't worry."

"Is it something about Jack? It is, isn't it?"

He sat beside her and took both of her hands in his.

"Eli, tell me! Has something happened to Jack? Is he hurt?"

"No. He's not hurt." he spoke softly, "He's doing very well."

"That's a good thing, isn't it? I don't understand."

"He's living in New York."

"That's good! Now we know where we can find him!"

"That's just it, Syd. He doesn't want to be found. He...seems to have built a whole new life for himself."

"What does that mean?"

"He...He was spotted with Stephen Browne at a gay establishment...and they looked cozy...very cozy."

Her face collapsed into itself and her delicate features crumpled up like tissue paper.

"Then, he does remember me...and he chooses to stay away from me..."

"Sydney, I wish there could've been a better way to break this to you."

"That was my last shred of hope...If he regained his memory, he'd come back to me. I was a big fool to think he'd still want to be with me."

"No, Syd, he's the fool." he embraced her, "The biggest fool in the world."

"At least, now, I have certainty." she said, "No more questions, no more hopes or dreams. This time, I know without a doubt that it's over. He's moved on without me, and I have to find a way to move on without him."

"And you will. You'll move on and find someone who wants only you and no one else."

"I doubt that, but I'll find a way to get on with my life somehow."

"That's the girl." he stroked her cheek.

"It could've been a lot worse. He could've chosen another woman. That would've hurt much more. At least, he was considerate enough to choose a man over me."

For now, she just needed to remain here in her safe haven with Eli, and allow her tears to wash away every trace of the imagined life she would never know.

Eli jumped at the sound of the telephone.

"I'll just check who it is. I won't be long." he picked up the receiver promptly to silence the caller, "Hello. Oh, yes...She's right here, Brett. I'll put her on." Eli handed her the receiver.

"Sweetheart, are you all right?"

"It's so good to hear your voice, Brett! You've heard about it, too?"

"It's all over the news, hun: The local paper, the radio, T.V....Are you all right?"

"Hanging in there, with a lot of help from Eli."

"I'm glad he's there for you, sweetheart. I wish I could be with you, too."

"I miss you, Brett."

"I miss you so much, hun, I can't see straight. I can't wait to see you."

"Me, too."

"Are you still coming for Dottie's grad?"

"Wouldn't miss it for anything in the world."

"Take good care of yourself, sweetheart. I know you're in good hands with Eli."

"You take good care, too, Brett. I love you."

"I love you, too, sweetheart."

"Please give my best to everyone."

"I will. Stay strong, baby. Love you."

"Love you."

Handing the receiver back to Eli, she smiled in gratitude. She was blessed to have the two of them as her friends. It was time to release Jack and wish him well on his journey – a journey that no longer included her.

* * *

"You're too soft, Rosie." Mike shook his head. "The guy was a fraud. He fooled all of us. I've got no sympathy for him."

"Have a heart, Mike." she wiped her tears on her greasy apron, "The poor boy was terrified. I could tell there was something special about him. I knew he was a sensitive, tortured soul."

"Don't waste your tears on him. He's done just fine for himself now. Think about the people he's hurt. I always knew there was something shifty about that boy."

"He don't know who he is or what he wants."

"Sure looks like he found out now." Mike laughed, soon joined by Lou and Ed.

"I'm going to miss him." Rosie sniffled. "I hope he finds the peace he deserves."

"How about letting us have some peace, Rosie?" Mike roared with laughter, prompting the other man to join him.

Rosie hung her head and returned to the customers.

* * *

Ribby pulled Cicely into a bone-crushing embrace.

"Oh, my honey child!" she patted her back maternally.

"Thanks for coming over, Ribby." Cicely produced a tissue from the pocket of her quilted yellow robe and dabbed at her eyes, "It was all a lie. He never cared about me."

"Oh, honey, I think he cared. He cared deeply about you."

"He doesn't even like women!"

"Six wives and a fiancée don't exactly indicate a man who doesn't like women. There's more to this than meets the eye."

"What are you saying, Ribby?"

"I'm thinking maybe, this Stephen fellow took advantage of his vulnerable state and told him a pack of lies. Maybe he had his eye on him when they knew each other before, but didn't get anywhere with him. So, when he saw an opportunity to exploit him, he thought all his Christmases came at once."

"That makes a lot of sense. Maybe he did care about me on some level. I guess deep down, I always knew it was temporary anyway, until he got his memory back and went back to be with his wife."

"Just remember him the way he was, honey. Remember the lovable, earnest man who came into your life for a brief time and made you smile. Hold that in your heart."

"Thank you, Ribby. You always know how to make me feel better. I'll put on the coffee."

"I can't stay too long, honey. I have to take Swandra and Shawndra to dance class today. Shanise got called in to work an extra shift because someone called in sick, so it's Grandma to the rescue. I do have enough time for a quick coffee, though. We can get caught up on all the gossip at the hospital. You'll have to fill me in on what's been going on. It's hard to keep up since I retired."

* * *

Car horns on Park Avenue were in aggressive competition with Barbra Streisand's heartfelt rendition of "I Didn't Know What Time It Was" on the phonograph. The relentless stream of tears fell, staining his blue satin bow tie. This enchanting song haunted his dreams every night...dreams of holding Sydney in his arms in a deserted nightclub. Sydney...Why couldn't he remember her? And why, despite his lack of recollections, was he filled with this inexplicable longing for her?

"You didn't love any of them." Stephen had told him, "You married all of them for cover. Being suspected of being gay would have been professional suicide."

He did not remember any of the others. Blurred faces, jumbled, mismatched names...No captured moments, no feelings...Only this inescapable snapshot of Sydney seared his soul.

"Ready, Sweet Cheeks?" he heard Stephen's voice from the living room, "I'm sure Johnny Cantrell wouldn't want to keep his fans waiting."

"I'll be right there, honey." he called out in a trembling voice.

"I'll go down and hail a cab."

This life of opulence had taken him hostage in its bejewelled prison. A new name. A new identity. A new lover. A new residence. But who was Jack Chandler? For now, he was Johnny Cantrell, a weary lounge singer, the companion of a successful advertising executive. He wanted desperately to surrender his heart to Stephen completely but he was much too aware that could never be. Sydney would always loom larger than life between them.

The magnificent lights of New York City melted like grotesque candles behind the rain-streaked windows of the cab. He shivered. The warmth of Stephen's hand over his own ice-cold hand was soothing. How could he be such a wretch to take such affection for granted? He was the luckiest man to possess the kind of love others only dreamed about.

On the stage, facing a sea of strangers, catching Stephen's loving gaze from the front row stirred his heart. Halfway through his set, he observed Kent and Aydin had joined Stephen at his table. They appeared to be embroiled in a heated discussion. He concluded his set with "Long Ago And Far Away" and retreated to his dressing room, unnoticed. Later, outside the back door, he caught sight of them as they waited for him, still engaged in their intense interaction. He ducked behind a parked van to listen undetected.

"You can't keep this up any longer; you know it's wrong." he could hear Aydin's voice.

"If you don't come clean, I'm going to do it for you." Kent said.

"You're exploiting him. This deception has to end." Aydin stated.

"I've waited a lifetime to be with Jack. I never imagined fate would bring him back into my life like this. How can I let him go now?"

The group was then approached by two women and hugs were exchanged all around. Jovial pleasantries ensued. He approached the group tentatively.

"There you are! We were worried about you." Stephen turned to him.

"Sorry, I got talking with a chap and lost track of time." he could sense the love in Stephen's eyes.

"This is Vivian." Aydin nodded toward the raven-haired woman, "And this is Mara."

"Very pleased to meet you." the red-haired woman shook his hand enthusiastically.

"It's nice to finally meet you." Vivian said.

"Very nice to meet you both." he smiled.

"Well, we have to get home. Tomorrow's a work day for some of us. See you guys later."

"See you ladies later." Kent said. "We have to get going ourselves."

"Take care, Jack." Aydin cast a solicitous glance at him, softly touching his shoulder.

"Thanks, Aydin. You, too."

"Good night, Jack." Kent said and led Aydin away, shooting a stern glance at Stephen.

"Let's go home and have some brandy to warm up." Stephen placed an arm around him.

He was wanted. This was where he belonged. And where he intended to stay.

Chapter 15/ HEART OF MINE

She shifted uncomfortably in her white wrought-iron lawn chair. There was little leg room at the table the four of them were sharing. Taking great pains to avoid Lea's knees under the table, she kept her legs in an unnatural position. She was turned slightly to her right toward Brett, to avoid touching Tony's legs on her left, as well. Lea's cold, scrutinizing eyes had not left her face the entire time. Despite Brett's painstaking attempts to initiate a four-way conversation, a tense silence continued to hang over them. Once the staff cleared the dishes, they put on music. Dottie and J.T. were the first ones on the dance floor. Soon, they were joined by Annette and Donald, and their invited guests. Sydney kept her head down to avoid eye contact with her mother's sister and her husband. Her parents had declined Dottie's invitation, to keep the peace. She now regretted not doing the same. When Willard and Mildred took to the dance floor under the colorful patio lanterns, she turned her back to the dancing couples.

"Please don't mind my back, Tony." she whispered, "I'm sure you understand my reason."

"Don't worry about it." he reassured her.

"Tony, dance with Sydney." Brett said.

"I can't..." she protested.

"Yes you can." Brett persisted.

"Brett, no. No offense, Tony. I'm sure you know why."

"Forget about them and dance with me."

She smiled uncomfortably and allowed him to help her up and lead her to the dance floor. They were playing an orchestral version of "A Lover's Concerto". He swept her up in his arms and pressed her close. His heart was beating in her own chest. His neck smelled of waterfalls and sun-drenched meadows. She hoped he would not hear her heart beating fast. When the song ended, she lowered her eyes.

"Let's stay for the next song." he said as they started playing "All The Things You Are". "See? They're playing all your favorites."

She smiled and complied. When the song ended, he whispered in her ear:

"Syd, there's something I have to talk to you about. Why don't we take a little walk on The Green?"

She nodded in agreement. He took her arm and led her around the side of the house.

"Is something wrong?"

"No, nothing major. I just wanted to tell you about some changes that I needed to make before construction is complete for the club. There's been so much public backlash that I had no choice but to change the name of the club. For obvious reasons, it can't be called "Jack's" anymore."

"I understand."

"I'm thinking of calling it "Aurelie's". I wanted to run it by you."

"It's a lovely choice. But, Tony, you don't have to run anything by me; you're the sole owner now. All decisions are yours alone."

"I don't want to do anything to disrespect you, Sydney."

"I appreciate that. You're very considerate, Tony. Thank you."

"You're a lovely lady. I would never do anything to hurt you."

"Thank you...Do you think we should head back?"

"There's no hurry. I don't think they're going to miss us."

"It's a beautiful night for a walk. And it was getting too stuffy back there. Dottie must be happy to be all done with school. Does she have immediate plans?"

"I don't think so. She doesn't care about anything except J.T." he laughed softly.

"I'm very happy for her. I hope he treats her well."

"He seems like a nice enough fellow. I guess time will tell. What about you? How are things in Toronto? Are you planning to stay in Beavertown a while longer?"

"I don't know anything for certain yet. It's all up in the air for now. I'll see how things go here."

"Why don't we get a coffee at "The Queen's" coffee shop?"

"That sounds nice." she smiled.

"It's probably the only place that will serve us. All the other coffee shops would refuse to serve us for being overdressed. "

"Only in New Brunswick." she laughed.

"Don't you miss all the quirky customs? No, don't answer that." he squeezed her arm.

They exchanged knowing glances and continued walking arm in arm.

* * *

She pressed the doorbell and waited for what felt like an eternity. A face peeked out from the tiny square of glass. The door opened; a dark-haired woman stood before her in a short burgundy negligee, vacantly staring at her, a bottle of vanilla musk massage oil in her hand. Her expression was of indifference and ennui.

"Yes?"

"Gabie, who's at the door, dear?" Brett's voice could be heard from the stairs.

"No one."

Sydney caught a fleeting glimpse of Brett at the bottom of the stairs, in a black merry widow corset with garters and black fishnet stockings.

"Whatever you're peddling, we don't want any." Gabie spoke sternly in her melodious French accent and shut the door in her face.

Sydney ran frantically through Wilmot Park, blinded by her tears. Behind her, she could hear her name being called. Was she imagining it? She turned around for an instant. Off in the distance, a frantic figure was in pursuit – black trench coat thrown haphazardly over her lingerie, voluminous hair bouncing in total abandon.

"Sydney! Sydney – please don't go! Sydney, please come back!"

Sydney quickened her steps until she was certain she was out of Brett's field of vision. Brett returned, defeated, hanging her head and wiping her tears and her nose on her coat sleeve.

"Who was that?" Gabie was waiting in the foyer.

"Why didn't you ask her in?"

"I didn't want anyone disturbing us. This is our rare time alone with that pesky Lea out of the way."

"But it was Sydney."

"Forget her. She's a loser."

"I've lost her. She's gone."

"She's history. You have me."

"I can't lose her now."

"You sure have some weird friends, cherie."

"I have to find her."

"You can't have it both ways, Brett, cherie. It's either me or her."

"Sydney's not a lover. You know that. She's the dearest friend I've ever had. I can't lose her."

"Are you sure you two were never lovers?"

"We've been through this before, Gabie."

"You're not too convincing, cherie. This reaction from you...And the reaction from her when she saw me...People don't act this way when they're just friends."

"You wouldn't understand."

"No, I understand very well. Brett, I'm not a woman who likes to share. When you are with me, you must belong to me heart, body and soul. I tolerate nothing less. I gave you the best sex you've ever had in your life."

Unaware of Gabie's ramblings, Brett poured herself a scotch and drank it in one swig.

"My God, what have I done?" she sank on the sofa and buried her face in her hands.

"This is *incroyable!*" Gabie exploded, "A beautiful, vital woman like you, wasting your time thinking about a pathetic nobody like her! You should be counting your lucky stars you've got me in your life."

"I can't breathe without Sydney. She's my rock, my foundation. She's the reason I'm able to face another day."

"This is way too creepy for me. I thought you were somebody. I guess I was wrong. You can go back to your precious Sydney."

Unaware of Gabie's presence, Brett fell to the floor, sobbing, calling out Sydney's name.

"You repulse me." Gabie stepped over her legs and ran up the stairs.

Brett crawled on her hands and knees to the bar. With great difficulty, she scrambled to her feet and hugged the bottle of Grant's scotch to herself. She sank to the floor, leaning her back against the side of the cabinet. She opened the bottle, lifted it to her lips and let the nectar soothe her parched throat. Gabie descended the staircase fully dressed, and suitcase in hand.

"Don't bother to get up and see me out." she eyed Brett in disdain, "I don't think you can, anyway. You're nothing but a lush. An old lush. A has-been. I don't know what I ever saw in you. I can't believe you're the woman I idolized from afar all this time.

You're all washed out. And you're no superstar in bed, either. I've wasted my time here. While you were fucking me, you wanted to be fucking her. You two losers deserve each other!"

Brett heard the slamming of the door. She threw down the bottle and rose to her feet, leaning against the cabinet. She tossed her coat on the floor and staggered up the stairs. Standing before the streaked mirror over the stained white sink, she did not recognize the woman looking back at her. She splashed cold water on her face. She knew what she needed to do.

* * *

Her martini tasted distinctively of vermouth. Noticing her empty glass, the middle-aged bartender approached her with a congenial smile.

"Another martini, please. This time, more gin and less vermouth." she said.

"This was your tenth martini, Contessa."

"It doesn't count. You've been watering them down." she asserted. "All I can taste is vermouth."

"You're going to be awfully sick tomorrow morning. Wouldn't you rather switch to a soft drink?"

"I would rather have another martini, please – this time a proper martini with more gin and less vermouth."

"I've never seen a woman drink like this before: Ten martinis – one right after the other."

"Technically, I only had a couple of martinis; the rest were mainly vermouth."

"I'll bet you could drink any man under the table." he shook his head. "You don't even seem tipsy."

"I'm not. Just keep 'em coming, buddy."

"Trying to drown your sorrows?"

"Something like that."

"Why do you bother drinking if it has no effect on you?" he sounded genuinely intrigued.

"I'm hoping, if I have enough, it's eventually going to kick in."

"You'll get sick before you get drunk."

"I don't get sick from gin. I only get sick from wine and sweet, syrupy drinks."

"You're an intriguing lady, Contessa." he winked flirtatiously at her.

She regarded the tall, dark-haired man with suspicion. He appeared to be her age – perhaps a year or two older – well-built, and self-assured.

"I hope you're not planning to drive home."

"No. I'm not driving."

"I'm off duty in fifteen minutes. I can drive you home, if you like."

"I'm not going home. I'm planning to stay at this motel for the night."

"Would you like company? I'm a good listener."

"No thanks. I'll be fine."

"Suit yourself, then, Contessa. If you change your mind, I'll be around for a while after I get off work. But no more martinis. I'm going to bring you a club soda now with a twist of lemon."

"You drive a hard bargain." she smiled.

"You should smile more, pretty lady."

She did not see Tony burst in through the door and make a beeline in her direction.

"There you are! I'm glad you're okay!" he placed both hands on her shoulders.

"Tony, what are you doing here?"

"Brett called me and asked me to look for you."

"How did you know where to look?"

"She said you were running in the direction of Sunshine Gardens. This was the most logical place to look."

"I'm sorry you went to all the trouble for nothing. As you can see, I'm just fine." she held up her glass. "I'm enjoying my lovely club soda here."

"Is this man bothering you, Contessa?" the bartender was scowling, "I can kick him out, if you want."

"No, he's a friend." she patted Tony's arm.

"Come on, let's get a table, so we can speak properly." Tony said, "I'll settle the bar tab." he called out to the bartender as he led her away.

"You don't have to babysit me, Tony. I'm sure you're tired after a full day at work. There must be better things you could be doing."

"I'm here because I want to be. I know this whole thing with Jack is still quite raw; you need time to process it. It's understandable you'd get upset and run off when Brett brought him up. It's going to take time to heal from this. I want you to know I'm here for you."

"It's very kind of you."

"We're friends – and I want to be here for you. It might be easier to talk to a man about this. You and Brett are too close, so it's hard for her to be objective. She didn't mean to demonize Jack and upset you, but she hates what he's done to you."

She nodded in agreement.

"I do have to call Brett and let her know I've found you safe and sound. I got a late start. I was at a meeting when she called the office. By the time I got her message and called her back, she was going out of her mind."

"I'm sorry to be so much trouble for both of you."

"That's what friends are for, Sydney." he touched her hand, "I won't be long."

He motioned to the other bartender, the ponytailed younger man.

"I'd like to use the phone, please."

"Yes, Mr. Horncastle." the young man placed the mustard yellow bar phone within his reach.

"Thanks." he dialed the number, aware of the older bartender's stern glance. "Hi, Brett. I found her...Yes, she's all right. At the Admiral...Yes, I'll stay with her...Won't let her out of my sight...Don't worry...I'll call you when I get her home. Bye."

Exchanging daggers with the older bartender, he thanked the younger man and returned to the table.

"Let's get some black coffee first, and have a meal." he suggested. "You need to get food and coffee into you after all that booze."

"I'm not really hungry." she protested.

"I know, but you need to eat. Do you like pineapple chicken? Sure you do." he motioned to a nearby waitress, who promptly appeared at their table, "The lady will have the pineapple chicken, and chicken fried rice. I'll have the beef and broccoli with beef fried rice. The meals come with eggrolls, don't they?"

"Yes sir."

Once the server left, he observed that Sydney's eyeliner was smudged, lending her the haunted look of a burlesque dancer from a bygone era. The temptress who had captivated Jack and Warren was once again close enough for him to inhale the intoxicating scent of her skin. He wondered what she was like in bed. His thoughts had meandered in that direction from time to time for years. Now, here she was: Vulnerable and alone. He despised himself for entertaining such thoughts, yet it appeared fate had brought the two of them together under these painful circumstances. And who was he to question that?

Chapter 16/ IT'S MY TURN

"Let's go for a walk." he held the door open for her.

"Tony, I'm sure you've got better things to do. I don't want to keep you any longer."

"It'll do you good to get some fresh air." he removed his suit coat and helped her put it on.

She did not protest. Crisp spring air caressing her face, and feeling the gentle pressure of his arm linked through hers, she held her breath, afraid he might vanish if she exhaled. They strolled in silence through the sleepy streets of immaculate post-war Colonial-revival homes.

"I've always wanted to live in Sunshine Gardens." he mused.

"So have I." she looked up in astonishment, "It's the perfect neighborhood."

"I don't care for the newer places up the hill. They're just cheaply built cookie-cutter bungalows."

"You could buy a house here, so when your daughter visits, she'll have a nice backyard to play in."

"I think I already missed the boat, Sydney."

"You never know."

"Yes. You never know...Are you cold? Do you want to go back?"

"I'm all right, but you must be cold in just your shirt."

"I'm fine, but we should probably head back. I still have to call Brett."

"You're right."

He followed her up the outdoor stairs to the second floor balcony of the motel. She unlocked her door.

"This is it." she stepped aside to showcase the room with a sweep of her arm.

"Looks like they've updated the décor." he remarked, "I expected to see putrid orange from the seventies, but this is actually quite tasteful."

He crossed the room to the desk and dialed the sage green rotary dial phone.

"Hi...It's me...She's home safe and sound. Now, I'm going to turn in for the night myself. It's been a long day...No problem. We'll talk tomorrow. Good night." he hung up.

"One of these days, " Sydney smiled wickedly, "Someone's going to invent a phone that shows what number you're calling from...and you're going to be so busted."

"By that time, we'll all be dead and gone."

"Unfortunately so, but I wish I could watch you squirm your way out of these situations with a 'tell-all' phone." she laughed.

"Wow, I didn't see that coming. There's a dark, sadistic side to Sydney Goldstein no one ever suspected." he winked, "I'd better watch my step around you."

"Now that you've inspected my room and lied to Brett about where we are, you can go home and get some much-needed rest, Tony." she handed him his suit coat, which he tossed on the floor.

"You don't have to be so stubborn, you now. No one can be strong all the time. Sometimes, we need someone to lean on, Sydney."

"Tony..."

"I want you to lean on me. I want to be here for you."

"You don't have to, Tony. You've been exceptionally kind and gracious, but I'll be fine alone."

"I have no intentions of leaving you alone tonight, Sydney." he stated with a furrowed brow.

"Tony, we've been through all this. I'm too tired to argue with you anymore."

"Then, don't." he swept her into a fervent kiss.

She moaned and fumbled blindly with his tie. She managed to whip it off and toss it at their feet. Tugging frantically at his shirt, she kissed him with unexpected desire. His skillful fingers were working their way over her body, effortlessly removing her clothing.

"Oh, God, Sydney, I want you so much!" he threw her down on the bed, "I've wanted you for so long."

"I want you, too." she pulled him down and bit his earlobe.

She opened herself up to him. Waves of ecstasy banished all visions of Brett with Gabie, and Jack with Stephen. She could easily become addicted to Tony's lovemaking.

"Any regrets?" he asked, as they lay beside each other in the afterglow.

"No regrets." she murmured. "Tony, I don't want you to leave – ever." she placed her head on his chest.

"I won't. I'll never leave you, Sydney."

"Please stay with me here for another night."

"I'll stay as long as you want me to."

"Tony, I want you to know this is not a rebound thing for me."

"The way you made love to me already told me that." he kissed her hair.

Tony smiled to himself. Sydney was his, at last. Warren and Jack had not appreciated her and lost her, but he would never make that mistake.

* * *

Warren found Lea on the porch swing in the sunroom, with the sleeping Aurelie's pram nearby.

"Who let the wind out of your sails, Mademoiselle?" he closed the door behind him.

"Jezebel."

"And, by Jezebel, you're referring to?"

"You know who I'm referring to: Princess Sydney."

"And, what has Sydney done to irk you?" he smirked.

"She spend the night with Tony; that's what."

Warren burst into laughter.

"And, you know this because Tony keeps you up to date on his dalliances?"

"Brett and I figured it out when I went to see her this morning."

"I didn't realize you ladies were clairvoyants."

"We compared notes and came to the obvious conclusion. Brett sent him after her yesterday because Sydney was upset when she caught Brett in a compromising position with Gabriele."

"This just gets better and better!" he roared with laughter, "Go on."

"He told Brett last night he took Sydney home and he was coming home himself, but when Brett phoned Sydney's parents this morning, Edna told her Sydney hadn't been home all night. Tony didn't come home last night, either. His assistant phoned the house looking for him this morning because he hadn't shown up for his appointments."

"Tony, you old devil you." Warren smirked, "Good for him. He'd been lusting after her for a long time. I didn't think he'd ever get her in the sack. I must congratulate him when I see him."

"Warren, this is serious."

"Of course it is. Tony takes matters of the heart very seriously."

"We can't let him get involved with that slut."

"I knew it was only a matter of time before she got around to fucking Tony. She's already been with me and Jack. It's only fair Tony doesn't get left out."

"I don't know why you're not taking this more seriously."

"He's a grown man, Lea. He knows what he's getting into. He knows her history. I think he's probably more suited to her than Jack and I were. Turns out Jack did her a favor by setting her free."

"I don't understand what it is about her that you men find so irresistible."

"That's because you're not a man."

"What's so special about her? I know she's pretty, but pretty women are a dime a dozen."

"You wouldn't understand."

"What I want to know is: How do you men know if a woman's good in bed if you haven't slept with her yet? Are there some secret signals or something?"

"It's all done with smoke signals." he laughed.

"I suppose there's a silver lining after all, though. She and Brett are on the outs now because of Gabriele."

"Those two can't stay away from each other for long. Don't get too comfortable in Brett's bosom, Lea. They'll be thick as thieves again in no time."

"Not if I can help it. I won't let her swoop back in and hurt Brett again. She uses people and throws them away. Then, she moves on to her next victim."

"This dark image you've painted of Sydney as a femme fatale just cracks me up."

"It's 'femme'." she enunciated slowly, "It doesn't rhyme with phlegm, but rhymes with bum."

"You must be a real fun teacher." he laughed, "The kids must love you…Rhymes with bum. How could anyone forget that? By the way, tell me more about this Gabriele. Is she Brett's latest conquest?"

"They're over now, as far as I know. Gabriele got mad and walked out on Brett when Sydney showed up."

"Hmmm…Another love triangle. Better watch out, Lea: Sydney's going to fuck Brett next." He bent over with laughter.

"You find all this amusing, don't you?"

"I find it hilarious."

"You're a very strange man; you know that?"

"Why, thank you, Mademoiselle. I'll take that as a compliment."

"You're incorrigible."

"Lea, I'm really going to miss all the entertainment you provide around here." he walked out, casting a quick glance at her scowling face.

* * *

In the stillness of early morning, the pool known for notorious parties appeared deceptively calm. Wrapped in the peach floral bedspread, she sipped coffee from a white cup.

"Why don't you come back to bed?" he called out to her, placing his coffee cup on the nightstand.

She turned away from the window, crossed the room and let the cover fall to the floor.

"I can't get enough of you." he gazed tenderly at her, "I don't want you to go back to Toronto yet. I miss you already."

"I don't want to be away from you for one minute, Tony. I want to stay in your arms forever. I wish we could shut the rest of the world out."

He pulled her closer and kissed her forehead.

"We can. I'm going to rent an apartment in Toronto and arrange to take time off from work, so we can be together. I'll try to get away as often as I can. Then, when you feel it's safe for you to come home, we'll announce to the whole town we're a couple."

"Tony, are you sure you want to risk a public lynching for being with an outcast like me?"

"Sydney, you're not an outcast. Everything'll blow over soon." he kissed her hand, "Do you have any idea how much I love you? I would never let anyone hurt you."

"I love you, too, Tony. I can't imagine my life without you."

"You never have to." he held her, feeling her trembling body, and soothed her with soft kisses.

* * *

"Congratulations, my boy." Warren greeted him in the atrium.

Tony frowned quizzically.

"For bagging the prize." Warren winked.

Tony appeared perplexed.

"I found out from Lea."

"Lea? How did she…"

"Never mind. Long story. I'll tell you later. She's a busybody. I'm proud of you."

"It wasn't like that. She's much more than a roll in the hay. I love Sydney. I want a future with her."

"I think you'd be good together. I mean that. I hope everything works out."

"I appreciate that, Warren. Coming from you, it means a lot."

"I hope she loves you, too."

"She does. Jack is out of her system now."

"I hope you're sure about that. If Jack waltzed back into her life and asked her to take him back, would she choose you over him? I don't want you to get hurt again."

"I'm willing to take that chance."

"I hope she doesn't let you down. I just want you to be sure about making a commitment. Sydney's great in the sack and she's a captivating, passionate woman, but you need to tread carefully. She's also very complex."

"I wanted to be with her long before Jack turned her head with his boyish charm and sad eyes. But I respected the fact that they were a couple. I supported them in every way. Then, Jack pulled this stunt with Stephen."

"I'm not trying to burst your bubble, but I don't think any of that stuff is true. I don't believe he has his memory back and has chosen Stephen over her. I've always thought that Stephen was a dodgy sort. I'm concerned that if Jack does get his memory back, he'll come right back here to be with her."

"Hopefully, by that time, all the feelings she had for him will be gone."

"Sydney will choose you, even if her heart wants Jack. She will do the right thing. I know her. But you deserve a woman who loves you with all her heart."

"I'll cross that bridge when I get to it. At any rate, this might be a moot point. Jack might never get his memory back. It doesn't seem likely with this Stephen latching onto him."

"I can't wait to see the look on old Willy's face when he finds out." Warren smirked.

"I don't even want to think about that."

"Are you going to talk to Brett?"

"There's no need. She redefined our boundaries when she found out about Lea's pregnancy. We've been just platonic friends since."

"Not too many could've done what the two of you did for those eight years, maintaining such fluid boundaries."

"Brett's an extraordinary woman."

"That's one way of putting it."

"I think she'd be happy for us."

"I think so, too. But proceed with caution, nephew: Sydney is a very damaged woman. There are things none of us might ever know about her."

"That is not an issue for me. I know she tries to be strong and keep it together, but she's very fragile."

"I want to give you a heads-up about something Lea told me: I don't think either Sydney or Brett have told you. The reason Sydney left Brett's house in a frantic state and drank like a sailor that night was catching Brett in a compromising position with another woman."

"You mean Lea?"

"No. Not her! To me this is a red flag."

"I don't have a problem with that. I'm sure she was too confused and embarrassed to tell me. She's probably still trying to sort it in her mind. All her life, people have let her down. I want to be the one who treats her the way she deserves to be treated."

"It's very noble of you. You want to rescue her; you want to be her hero. It's a pattern with you: You seek out damsels in distress. Adele was an ex-nun trying to find her way; Brett was a divorcee with children, trying to make ends meet. But, this time, you've really outdone yourself: Sydney's a social pariah. And, she's bedded two members of your family."

"She's the love of my life. A rare gem. And I'm not going to let her get away."

165

"We'll discuss this further, at a later time, nephew. I think I hear someone coming." he patted him on the shoulder.

Tony ascended the stairs to his suite with slow, weary steps.

* * *

"You've been a busy girl, Madame." he called out to her in her parents' driveway.

"It's not anything sordid."

"I know. I just want to be sure you're as committed as Tony is."

"Of course I am."

"What if Jack turned up out of the blue and wanted you back?"

"Jack is my past. Tony's my present and future."

"Wouldn't you feel torn, even a little bit?"

"No. I love Tony. Yes, a part of me will always love Jack, just as a part of Tony will always love Brett, but I'm committed to Tony."

"You're going to meet harsh opposition from his parents. They're going to crucify you."

"I know what they put Brett through years ago."

"Tony attempted to take his own life when they came between them and prevented them from getting married. That's why the two of them carried on an unconventional arrangement for so many years."

"I'm aware of all that, Warren. His parents don't scare me. I'm prepared to take them on. They have no right to interfere in his life."

"You never cease to amaze me." he shook his head in disbelief, "I just want you to know, if you hurt Tony, you'll answer to me."

"You don't have anything to worry about, Warren." she looked him straight in the eye, her mouth in a taut line.

She knew, from the softened look in his eyes, that she had his blessing.

Chapter 17/ INNOCENCE

Marin took her place in line behind the short woman in the silver raincoat. She had been admiring the satin crib mobile with the clouds and the rainbow for weeks now, each time she passed by the gift shop on her way home from the doctor's office. With only Sam working, and not even bringing in enough to live on comfortably, this was a luxury they could do without. No doubt, she would receive a tongue lashing from Sam for wasting hard-earned money on a frivolous purchase. Their dismal townhouse in a gritty, blue-collar enclave built over a swampland was furnished with cast-offs and hand me downs. Their Spartan existence provided no perks, and no release from the drudgery of their poverty. Now that it was about to become the three of them, Sam had become even more distant and short-tempered. He spent more evenings out with his friends. It seemed they fought more now, and always about money. She had contributed nothing to the marriage. Not for lack of trying: Every path she had chosen had led to peril.

The line was moving slowly. She would soon need to use the bathroom. She shifted her weight to her other foot. Hers had been an ideal pregnancy: No morning sickness, no hypertension, no complications, and moderate weight gain. She had grown comfortably into her ever-expanding abdomen. Everything about this pregnancy felt right. Bringing a child into the world had been a mutual decision. Girl or boy, this baby would be cherished.

She was finally able to pay for her purchase with cash she could not afford to spend. Outside the door, the gust of wind twisted her skirt around her thighs. She pulled it down furiously and struggled as she stumbled down the sharp incline of brickwork under foot.

Soon, Brett's SMT bus would be arriving at the terminal. She took a seat on a beat-up vinyl bench with a view of the door. Once a vibrant cherry red, the seat had faded to a coral. This old bus terminal would be closed in another year and a posh modern one blocks away would be taking its place. John's Bay was in the throes of urban renewal, making a concerted effort to shake off its industrial image. A stone castle which had been vacant for decades was recently converted to an upscale nightclub. Gift shops and tea rooms lined the old streets. Bar and grills with Formica counters and jukeboxes were being razed to make room for office space. The most tragic casualty was the beloved family-owned department store – a long-standing landmark which had been demolished to erect a modern shopping mall. She feared John's Bay would lose its urban character and old world charm. With its imperfections, its inferiority complex, and its filth, it was so desperately flawed, it could not help being astonishing and breathtaking.

She heard a gruff voice announce over the loudspeaker that the bus from Beavertown had arrived and would soon be departing for Truro, Nova Scotia. She rose, searching for Brett amid the crowd of passengers. Taller than almost everyone else, she was easy to spot.

"Mom!" Marin ploughed her way through the crowd.

"Sweetheart!" Brett pulled her close and kissed her cheek, "I missed you! How are you feeling?"

"Terrific, now that you're here! Welcome to my city of fog and stench."

"You're absolutely radiant." Brett pushed her blue tinted bifocals on top of her head, "Pregnancy really agrees with you."

"You look beautiful, Mom." she admired her blue print Laura Ashley dress.

"So do you, hon. My gorgeous daughter's about to become a mother herself. You'll be the best mother."

"I hope I can be like you."

Brett squeezed her gently. In her red gingham maternity dress, red canvas flats, and with her curls pulled away from her freshly-scrubbed face, Marin appeared like a child of twelve or thirteen. She longed to hold her close and shelter her from all harm, all abuse, all the inevitable pain that awaited her. She feared Lynn and Emerald both, and the tug of war that would erupt, pitting three grandmothers against one another. She had chosen to avoid conflict at all costs, even if it meant less access to her grandchild, for the sake of harmony in Marin's life. Lynn would sharpen her claws for Emerald and Emerald would play the martyr for Marin.

Emerald was still in the dark about Marin's knowledge of her true identity. Henry had found a way to protect his wife from the real world yet again. All of her friends were instructed by him to conceal the truth. Marin would continue to live under the pretense of being Acacia Leigh.

"I wish you didn't have to go back to Beavertown when I bring the baby home."

"Sweetheart, I'd give anything to be here to dote over my precious grandchild and help you out as much as possible, but Emerald expects to fill the grandmotherly role."

"That is your rightful territory."

"I don't want to cause trouble. She's a very troubled woman and there's no telling what she might be capable of if she finds out."

"I'm going to miss you, though."

"Me, too. As soon as Miss Emerald returns to Beavertown, I'll be on the first bus back here. I'll do everything to help take care of my grandchild."

"It's your company that matters, not what you do."

"We'll have all kinds of time together for now, hon. Do you have names picked out yet?"

"If it's a girl, I'm going to name her after you."

"Oh, sweetheart! You don't have to."

"I want my child to have your name."

"What about your dear grandmother and your Aunt Della? They deserve some sort of recognition. I don't want to take that away from them."

"I've thought of that: As a middle name, I'm going to combine their names: Noradell: Honor and Della together."

"Marin, that's ingenious! I'm honored. What if it's a boy?"

"Brett Seth Cullen."

"That's lovely."

"Why don't we have some cherry pie at the Woolworth's cafeteria before we take the city bus to the West Side?"

"Sounds good to me. You've got to feed the little one." she patted Marin's stomach.

One of the few remaining tributes to the city's past, Woolworth's limped on, despite a disfiguring facelift in the early seventies which concealed its brick façade with unsightly aluminum siding and a metal mansard roof. The interior remained mostly unchanged, still maintaining its mid-century charm with enormous plate glass windows, generously-sized display bins, wide aisles, a photo booth by the side door, and terrazzo stairs to the basement. The cafeteria was a sight to behold: A sweeping staircase leading to a balcony overlooking the main floor, dazzling with fifties charm. They settled into a booth with peach vinyl benches. The menus were slippery with grease. When Brett leafed through hers out of curiosity, she came across the illustration of an ice cream sundae with its maraschino cherry faded to a pink.

"Are their cheeseburger platters good?" she asked.

"I've never had one. I've only had snacks here."

"Why don't we have some lunch? My treat. They have Southern fried chicken, too. Might be greasy, but what the heck? It might be fun."

A waitress in a pink uniform approached them, pad and pencil in hand. She wore oversized peach-framed glasses, and her hair was pulled into a bun, covered with a hairnet.

"What will you ladies have?"

"I'll have the fried chicken. What about you, sweetheart?"

"I'll have the same."

"What would you like to drink?"

"I'll have iced tea."

"I'll have milk." Marin said, patting her stomach.

"And, for dessert, we'd like cherry pie." Brett added.

"A la mode?"

"Sure. Why not?"

"Yes, ma'am."

"Everything's going to be fine." Brett said once the waitress was gone, "I promise you."

Marin smiled in gratitude. Everything was all right, as long as Brett was around.

*   *   *

Smiling groggily, she reached her hand over the railing.

"You were terrific through it all." Brett squeezed her hand in her own, "Sweetheart, I'm so proud of you."

"Thank you, Mom. She's beautiful, isn't she?"

"She is the most beautiful sight in the world. Are you all right, sweetheart? I know you had a lot of pain after child birth."

"I'll be all right."

"You get some rest, my angel. I'll be back in the morning."

"Thank you, Mom."

"I'll send Sam back in, so you can say goodnight in privacy. I'll wait for him in the lobby."

"Goodnight, Mom."

"Goodnight, baby girl." she kissed her forehead.

The corridor was eerily silent. Middle-aged nurses slid past her, their silent rubber shoes in sparkling white, against the torn, aging, teal linoleum. The oily sheen of the teal alkyd paint on the walls heightened her sense of claustrophobia. She rode the elevator alone down to the lobby. With its high ceiling, orange upholstered chairs, stark white walls, and peach terrazzo floor with a black, white and green pattern of rectangular prisms, it was a spacious, welcoming lobby. Black and white photographs adorned the wall leading to a side corridor. She lacked the energy to walk the short distance to see them. Past the elevators was a turquoise-painted Virgin Mary statue.

The labor had been long and painful. Despite Marin's protests, the smirking anaesthetist, a short, smug young man, had ordered Marin to turn to her side and inserted what appeared to Brett to be a foot long hypodermic needle into her daughter's spinal cord. The epidural had done absolutely nothing to alleviate the pain. It had been topped up twice, still with only minimal pain relief. As she was being wheeled into the delivery room on a gurney, Marin began experiencing tremors and reached for her hand.

"Mom, what's happening to me?"

"It's the anaesthetic." a heavily made-up nurse explained coldly.

"Mom, don't leave me."

"Your mother has to wait out here. Only husbands are allowed in the delivery room."

"Please..."

"Too many people in the delivery room would only get in the way. She'll wait for you out here. You can see her after the baby's born and you've had your bed bath. And only for a few minutes. You need your rest. You can visit tomorrow."

"Don't worry, sweetheart. I'll wait right here. I'll pray for you." Brett reassured her.

Casting one final glance in Brett's direction, Marin was wheeled into the room, with Sam in tow. Brett wept, listening to desperate shrieks coming from the delivery room. Then, a baby's lusty cry rang out. She sighed in relief.

"It's a girl!" Sam announced jubilantly as the door opened.

Marin's gurney was wheeled out. Brett rushed to her side.

"Are you all right, baby?" she stroked her cheek.

"Isn't she beautiful, Mom?" she was nuzzling a tiny pink bundle, peeled back only slightly to reveal a plump face. "Welcome to the world, Brettiella Noradell Cullen."

Brett caressed her forehead with a fingertip. She observed that Marin was still quivering uncontrollably.

"You're a very lucky little girl, because you have the best mommy in the whole world." Brett said.

"Meet your grandmother, Brettiella." Marin said, "You are named after her. She is the best grandma in the world. I hope you are going to have a happy life, Brettiella. We all love you very much and I hope we can take good care of you."

"The baby needs to go to the nursery now." the nurse snatched the baby away, "And you have to get your bed bath. Your husband's the only one allowed to see you in the room. Your mom can visit tomorrow."

"No! I need to see my mom!"

"Those are the rules."

"It's okay, hon. I'll be back tomorrow. You get some rest. I love you."

"I love you, too."

"I'll wait for Sam in the cafeteria. We'll be back in the morning."

Nothing could have prepared her for this exhilaration, and this fear. She feared for her fragile granddaughter's life – heart of her heart – dearer than life itself. How would she be able to protect her from this ugly world? Would she live long enough to watch her grow into a young woman? To be filled with such awe, such joy, she believed her heart may burst out of her chest and explode before her eyes. She wanted to savor each breath, each moment of wonder.

She was grateful that Maggie had informed her about Mrs. Spinner, who knitted for a most reasonable fee for women like her with no gift for turning out exquisite baby layettes. No doubt, speed knitter Emerald had outdone her humble offerings. That was all right. She closed her eyes and said a silent prayer for Brettiella.

*　*　*

Toby crumpled the grimy, wrinkled sheet of paper he had retrieved from the mailbox and flung it into the wastepaper basket.

"Don't throw them away, Toby." Lea came out of the kitchen, drying her hands on her orange apron with white chickens across the bib. "It's evidence. I've been keeping a stack of them in my room for future reference. I intercept them so your mom won't see them. If things escalate to the next level, we'll need all the ammunition we can get."

"Shit!" he banged his fist against the wall after retrieving the crumpled paper, "Man, I'm so mad; I've been ripping up the ones I find and trashing them! Mom's plenty spooked already. I thought I was doing good, keeping them from her. I figured she'd seen enough of them already."

"You were thinking of your mom. Your heart was in the right place. But, from now on, if you find any when you come to visit, will you give them to me? I've already got plenty of them to use against him if we take the next step."

"Thanks, Lea. I'm glad you're here for Mom."

"This is the last thing she needs."

"If that pervert leaves another note, I'm going to deck him!" he swung his fists in the air.

"Abel Pearson is a very disturbed man, Toby. It's best to stay away from him."

"He's a pervert! All that sinner crap is getting old, man! 'You must repent for the life you're leading, you Jezebel.' Bullshit! Excuse the language."

"He's a religious zealot. I've seen his type before. I don't want to alarm you, but some are pretty dangerous. He's been bothering her on and off for a long time now – since the trial."

"I remember he used to stop her on the street and preach to her. She said she felt sorry for him because his wife is really sick, and she wouldn't tell the cops on him when he started writing the notes. Mom's such a softie."

"I don't think she saw him as a threat initially, but when these notes persisted, she got spooked."

"It's like he's watching her all the time. So what if Mom has a lot of boyfriends? She's a fox. That's what all the guys at school are saying. She's a modern woman, a fox, a babe. She's with it, not square like the other moms."

"I think he needs to be stopped. It's time to bring in the authorities."

"I wish they'd put Bibleman away forever. He's a menace. I see him passing out church pamphlets to little kids walking home from school. Trying to brainwash them at a young age. It's disgusting."

"I'll talk to your mom when she comes back from John's Bay and try to convince her to speak to the police and press charges."

"Man, I'm such a dufus!" he hit his forehead with his open palm, "What was I thinking? I threw away the evidence!"

"You can jot down the approximate times you found the notes you destroyed and try to remember as best you can, what they contained. Then, you can submit that to them."

"Cool! Lea, you're the greatest!"

"You're not too shabby yourself, lady killer." she tousled his hair, "Remember, not a word to a soul."

"I know. What's for supper, anyway?"

"Meatloaf and mashed potatoes with carrots and peas. I'm sorry that you have to eat boring food when both your parents are away."

"Hey, your cooking's great, Lea. That tourtiere you made the other day was the bomb. I like your chicken fricot, too. I'm getting cultured, eating French Canadian food."

"Thank you. Supper's in half an hour."

"I'll watch some T.V. until then."

Lea returned to the kitchen as Toby settled comfortably on the sofa.

* * *

They had lost Henry's phone number – the number at the house he would be staying in Nova Scotia. He would spend the next two weeks there on business, staying at a co-worker's home. The number he had written on the back of the paper bag containing Emerald's apples had disappeared from the kitchen counter. Marin did not remember disposing of it; neither did Sam. Emerald buzzed around like a hornet, with no consciousness of her actions, disposing of everything in sight, calling it 'ugly clutter'. She rummaged through the refrigerator, disposing of fruits and vegetables for reasons no one could fathom. She complained non-stop like a weed-whacker motor to anyone within earshot.

"That bed in your guest room is so uncomfortable." she announced to Marin on her first morning there. "I have a stiff neck and a sore shoulder. With my arthritis, I need a comfortable bed. I should be in your bed. You can take the guest room and Sam can sleep on the couch downstairs."

Marin leaned against the kitchen counter. The pain from her stitches had made it difficult to sit on any surface.

"I breastfeed Brettiella beside me on the big bed." was all she could say, praying Sam would put his foot down on this issue.

"Look at this food!" Emerald was temporarily distracted by another annoyance, "Your carrots are getting soft and your spinach is turning to mush; your potatoes are sprouting. You have jars that are past their due dates. You keep eating spoiled food, you'll get sick."

"I've been in the hospital having a baby, remember?"

"Teach your husband to take care of your food, then. I can't be here all the time, picking up after you!" she was frantically pulling jars and bottles out of the fridge and placing them by the sink, to be sorted later.

"Why don't you leave it? I'll sort them later."

"You never sort or clean anything! You live in a pigsty! You're not fit to be parents, the pair of you! Nothing but lazy slovenly trash. You live like animals. I can't believe you've brought a baby into the middle of this mess. You can't keep a clean house; you can't even take care of yourself. You're pathetic. I don't know how Sam can live with you. I feel sorry for that poor child you've created, having to grow up like this. I don't know where I went wrong. I raised you in a clean house. You're absolutely hopeless."

"Mama, you've got every surface covered with the contents of my fridge. How am I going to find something to eat for breakfast?"

"You're too fat to have breakfast. You have to go on a diet. I don't want an ugly fat pig for a daughter. Don't you have any self-control? Look at those hips! You're not eating as long as I'm staying here!"

"Mama, I'm breastfeeding. All I wanted was some fruit."

"You don't need it."

"I'm famished. I was up all night with the baby. She's colicky. She never slept at nights at the hospital, either. My stitches hurt like crazy when I use the bathroom."

"Still self-involved, I can see. All you think about is yourself. I'm inviting Barb Purcell here this afternoon and the place is a mess. Why don't you try to clean it up? I'm not your slave."

"Why do you want to invite company so soon?"

"I want some intelligent conversation. If I'm going to be cooped up in this dump for two weeks, I might as well make the best of it."

180

"I'm going to have a banana for energy."

"Bananas are full of calories! Why don't you try to make yourself presentable? I don't want Barb to see what a low-class slob I have for a daughter. Suck in your big gut. I told her when I invited her, you still look like you're about to give birth, so she won't be too shocked when she sees you."

"I don't know why we have to have company so early. I just got home from the hospital yesterday."

"Your neighbor Myrna dropped in yesterday. You had company. Now it's my turn."

"Myrna's not company. She was offering help. She's been there for me all through this pregnancy. She's been a Godsend."

"Well, I want my friend Barb to visit today. Get Noradell dressed in the yellow layette I knitted for her."

"Her name is Brettiella."

"That's a stupid name. I refuse to call my granddaughter by that woman's name. When are you going to outgrow these childish infatuations for women? It's revolting. I don't know how Sam can put up with you."

Marin turned to climb the stairs. Sharp pains were shooting down her right leg and folding it under like a wounded foal's. Pressing her weight against the wall, she staggered up the stairs. Once in her bedroom, she closed the door and dialed Myrna's number.

"What's wrong?" Myrna's chipper voice came on the line.

"How did you know something was wrong?"

"You've just had a baby. That's how. Tell me."

"Myrna, I can't walk. It hit me all at once. I barely made it up the stairs."

"You had an epidural, didn't you? I've heard you can have complications. You need to get some bedrest."

"I can't afford bedrest, Myrna."

"I think both you and the baby need to go back to the hospital, so you can get proper care. Call your obstetrician right now. I'll call Sam at work and tell him to come home and take you the doctor's office right away. Pack an overnight bag for the hospital."

"Thank you so much, Myrna."

"Leave your valuables at home."

"Mama's going to have a fit."

"Let her."

"She was planning to have a tea party with her friend this afternoon."

"Let her."

"She'll be mad that she can't show off Brettiella."

"Too bad for her. Listen, Marin, I'll get Sam to call the post office to have your mail rerouted here, so your mama doesn't find any envelopes addressed to 'Marin'. Sam can pick up the mail here on his way home from work. I have a feeling the doctor may keep you both at the hospital for quite a while. I'm going to call Sam now and you do as I said."

Marin followed Myrna's instructions and was told to meet her obstetrician at the hospital. She dressed promptly, bundled up Brettiella in warm clothing, and packed a bag. Downstairs, she could hear Sam's voice trying to reason with Emerald.

"What are you doing here?"

"I have to take Ma...Leigh to the hospital."

"There's nothing wrong with Leigh."

"She can't walk. The doctor wants her at the hospital."

"She's fabricating it to get attention. Leigh's still an immature child."

"She's experiencing complications from the epidural."

"What am I supposed to do here all by myself? You lost Henry's number. He can't come and get me."

"We have to get going. Honey!" he called up the stairs, "Are you ready to go? I'll come up and give you a hand."

"I can see she's got you wrapped around her finger."

"Hon, could you please come up and carry the baby?" Marin called down, "I'm afraid to carry her when I'm limping."

"Sure thing." he ran up the stairs two steps at a time.

"I'm worried." Marin handed the white, petal-soft fragrant bundle to him.

"It's going to be okay."

She limped behind him, all the while steadying herself with a palm against the wall.

Emerald was weeping downstairs.

"What am I going to do here stuck in a pigsty? Barb is the only friend I have in John's Bay."

"You'll be okay, Mama. We're off now."

The numbness that was so familiar to her when in the company of Emerald had taken up residence once again.

"Will you call Mom?" she asked Sam as they approached the surly older woman at the admissions desk.

"Brett's going to worry and want to come to John's Bay. Where is she going to stay?"

"I miss her. She's my mom. I know I'm being a sook."

"I'll call her and insist that she stay in Beavertown. I'll promise her frequent updates, but you know she won't be able to stay still. Knowing her, she'll hop on a bus here and check into a hotel."

"This whole thing is not fair. She's my real mom. She's the one who should be staying with us."

"I know it's not fair."

She was back in the Maternity Ward, this time in a room marked 'Isolation: Contaminated' reserved for the quarantined. Brettiella was back at the nursery. The attending nurse took Marin's vitals, asked pointed questions, and furiously took notes. Her examination also included checking her bleeding.

"Are you still wearing four pads?" the nurse asked in solicitude.

"I have to. I bleed through them so quickly."

"You shouldn't be bleeding that much by now."

"I didn't know. All they told me was that there would be a lot of bleeding. They didn't say how much or for how long."

"It should be lighter in amount and color by now. It should be pinkish, not red. Do you have abdominal pain?"

"All the time."

"You have a high fever. Both you and the baby have lost weight. You're too thin."

"Is something wrong with my baby?"

"No. You brought her in just in time, before it developed into a problem. Your milk isn't enough, so, she's lost weight. She'll need both breast milk and formula. We'll take good care of her. You, on the other hand, are another story. I don't mean to alarm you, but it's a lucky thing you came in because of your leg. You're hemorrhaging quite badly. It's pretty serious, you know."

"I...had no idea."

"You had a close call. Don't worry, we'll take good care of you. Your doctor's going to be here in a minute. He's already ordered a two week stay for the two of you. I'll inform him you're hemorrhaging, and he'll start you on an I.V. antibiotic like Gentamycin, which gets into the bloodstream quickly but not the breast milk."

Marin nodded her head sheepishly. Soon, Brettiella was brought in to see her, dressed in a ladybug print flannelette hospital gown, her white arms exposed like two tubes of marzipan. Her heart leapt in joy. Her little ladybug, that's what she would call her for a nickname. Ladybugs were good luck. Brettiella was her good luck charm. She closed her eyes and inhaled the vanilla scent of fresh skin. Brettiella pressed her smooth, round cheek on her mother's chest and glanced up with enormous knowing eyes. Safe in each other's warmth, mother and daughter drifted off to sleep.

Chapter 18/ ATONEMENT

"How's my favorite French teacher?" Warren found Lea in the atrium. "What new words are you going to teach me today?"

"C'est un jour merveilleux." Lea beamed, *"Parce que la putain est partie."*

"I don't have to be fluent in French to know what that means. But I wouldn't hold my breath if I were you, Lea."

"Now, things can go back to normal. They had their fling and got it out of their system."

"Don't get ahead of yourself, Mademoiselle. It wasn't a passing fancy. They're in a committed relationship now."

"He can't do that to us!"

"There's that 'us' again."

"Does that mean she's going to move back here?"

"Most likely."

"That's not fair!"

"All's fair in love and war, Mademoiselle."

"We have to break them up. You must know some femme fatales who can lure him away from her."

"I know some, but I don't know any that rhyme with 'bum'." he laughed.

"It's not funny. We can't let her move back here. Things were going along so nicely without her."

"C'est la vie."

"She'll monopolize all of Tony's time and all of Brett's time, too. I thought Brett would be upset with her for sleeping with Tony, but she doesn't seem the least bit troubled by it."

"I told you, they don't stay angry with each other for long."

"Maybe someone needs to have a talk with Tony's parents. Your entire family despises Sydney, so I think that would be an effective way to bring an end to this whole masquerade."

"I wouldn't advise that. You'd be opening a whole new can of worms, which would have devastating repercussions. If you care about Tony as much as I think you do, let sleeping dogs lie."

Taken aback by the expressions in his eyes, she fell silent.

"Lea, Sydney's not a threat to you. Her relationship with Tony is not going to deprive Aurelie from seeing her dad. I know her. She'd never want to be unfair or selfish. As for her friendship with Brett, distance is not going to have an impact on the intensity. It's something you'll simply have to accept. You're obsessing way too much over Sydney. If I didn't know better, I'd think you had a girl crush on her."

With a crimson face, Lea muttered unintelligibly under her breath in French.

"He'll be back from the airport soon." Warren said, "Stop scowling. Tony could've done a lot worse. You knew he'd get involved with someone. As much as you'd have liked to see it happen, he was never going to join a monastery. Any other woman would've restricted his daddy time and made demands from him to cause problems for all of you. I think you're going to find Sydney to be very reasonable to deal with. Thank your lucky stars." he walked away.

* * *

She turned on her hallway and kitchen lights and closed the door behind her. Her apartment was stuffy and damp. She opened the kitchen window. Too exhausted to unpack at this late hour, she carried her suitcase to the bedroom and deposited it in a corner. In the living room, she tossed her pocketbook and trench coat on the sofa and sat down. Closing her eyes, she rubbed her temples.

She could feel Tony's warm, moist flesh on her own, his tongue and fingers exploring uncharted regions, awakening desires no one had stirred before. Despite all his bravado, Warren had been no match for Tony in that department. Tony had an air of confidence without coming off as cocky. He was a patient, considerate lover. With his air of effortless sophistication and classic good looks, she had always thought of him as unattainable. Never in her wildest dreams had she imagined he could be attracted to her. No doubt he had been with countless women, all of them more worldly and more glamorous than her. Until that moment at the motel, she had considered his attention and concern as stemming from sympathy and friendship. But he desired her, too, and wanted a real relationship with her. She wondered what he could possibly see in her.

The sound of the telephone interrupted her reverie. Her heart leaped at the sound of his voice.

"Hello, gorgeous." he said.

"It's so nice to hear your voice, Tony."

"I wanted to make sure you got home safe and sound."

"I miss you already."

188

"I miss you, too. It won't be long. I'm working on getting it all arranged. I'll be with you very soon. I love you, Sydney."

"I love you, Tony."

"Sleep well, my beauty."

"You, too. You must be exhausted."

"I'll be dreaming about you all night."

"Me, too."

"Good night, darling. I love you very much."

"And I love you very much."

"I love you more. I'll let you go. Kisses."

"Kisses."

She smiled. In the morning, Eli would knock on her door and ask her about her trip, and share his wisdom with her. For now, she would allow herself the luxury of dreams.

* * *

"Every time I call Brett's number, that Lea girl answers the phone, so I hang up without saying a word. They probably think I'm a crank caller, but I don't know what else to do. Lea doesn't want me anywhere near Tony or Brett, and from what Warren has told me, she's on the war path right now."

"Why don't you give me the phone?" Eli stretched out his arm, "And write the number here." he nodded toward the notepad.

She complied and watched him as he dialed the number.

"Hello? Yes. I'm looking for Brett Morrow please. I'm from the telephone company. There's an issue with her last bill...Thank you." he winked at Sydney, "Brett? Hi, this is Eli. Just go along with me...Sydney's been trying to reach you, but your bodyguard's been giving her the brush-off, so can you please call her when the bodyguard is not around? You two need to have a good talk. If you can't get her at her number, try mine. She might be at my place...Thanks, Brett." he hung up.

"You're amazing." Sydney hugged him.

"You can't let Lea come between you."

"I need to make things right with Brett. I don't want this uneasiness between us."

"I agree. You two care far too much for each other to let this come between you."

She sighed in relief and went to the kitchen to plug in the tea kettle.

Chapter 19/ SINNERS

"Sweetheart, please don't cry like that!" Brett pleaded, "This breaks my heart. And I can't be there with you to give you a big hug."

"Brett, I'm so sorry...You can't imagine how bad I feel about the way I acted."

"You don't have anything to feel bad about, hon. I'm the one to blame."

"No! You're not to blame for anything."

"Why don't we just say no one's to blame and put it behind us?"

"Sounds good to me."

"Then, I want you to smile. Don't cry anymore. You know I love you. Let's forget about this."

"Okay."

"Oh, honey, I miss you."

"I miss you."

"I've been spending a lot of time in John's Bay lately."

"Is Marin feeling any better?"

"She's coming along. As long as Emerald stays away, she'll be fine. I tell you, that old witch is a piece of work."

"I can't believe she set up shop at Marin's house after she gave birth and abused her like that. Both Marin and

Brettiella were fighting for their lives and Emerald was complaining about being so bored all by herself."

"She's something else. I stayed with Chuck's cousin Nancy while Emerald was at their house. I was able to spend the days at the hospital with Marin and Brettiella. Marin loves the lilac dress you sent with Tony, by the way. She loves dressing up Brettiella in it for special occasions."

"I'm so glad she liked it. Brettiella must look beautiful in it."

"I'll send you some pictures with Tony. She's a beautiful baby."

"She comes by it naturally. Please give Marin my love."

"I will, hon. I'm glad you have Tony in your life now."

"That's something I wanted to talk to you about but I didn't know how to broach the subject."

"I really am happy for you, sweetheart. Tony is a strong, dependable man. That's what you need most."

"I wanted to be sure it was all right with you. If you have any reservations at all, you know I'd set him free. I don't want to cause trouble."

"Sydney, my sweet, don't ever think like that. I want you to be happy, and I know Tony can make you happy. You two are good for each other. You are exactly what he needs in a partner."

"Thank you, Brett. I don't know what to say."

"There's no need to say anything. I'm sorry Lea's been giving you a hard time. Tony told me she's been running off to Warren with tales of woe. In time, she'll get used to the way things are. I'll let you go for now, but I want you to smile for me, sweetheart. I love you."

"I love you so much, Brett."

* * *

"Aw, Mom, you're such a square!" Toby protested, "Microwaves are the latest trend. Everyone's got them! They're harmless!"

"I'm not really convinced that they are so harmless. All that radiation leak must cause cancer. Microwaves make me terribly uncomfortable."

"They've been around for years. Lotsa people have 'em. They're still alive."

"What's wrong with using a conventional oven?"

"Mom, get with the times. Microwaves can heat up your food in a couple of minutes. Regular ovens take twenty minutes."

"So, you put it in eighteen minutes earlier."

"Aw, Mom! This is the eighties!"

"Come here, you big lug!" she opened her arms to embrace him, "Give your mom a hug."

"Mom." he squirmed.

"Do you know how proud I am of you? My youngest, starting university. I'm going to miss you, but I know you need your freedom."

"Dad promised me and Keir a microwave, as long as you said it was okay."

"I guess I can't win this argument with you. Go on, then, go ahead."

"Thanks, Mom!" he hugged her, "I gotta go now. Keir and I are meeting a buncha guys at the 'Rollerama'."

"Have fun."

"Bye, Mom."

She followed him outside and stood watching him sprinting across Wilmot Park toward Sunshine Gardens, his blond hair glistening in the sun. Squirrels frolicked in the park in search of leftover crumbs from picnickers.

"It's hard to let go." a hand was on her shoulder.

Turning around, she found Lea standing behind her in an orange print tent dress.

"Hi, sweetheart. Where's my cute little lamb?"

"My parents are in town for a few days. They're taking her out in the stroller. I know it's hard for you now with both of the boys out of the nest. Someday, Aurelie will be testing her wings and going off on her own."

"They want a microwave, Lea. Josh promised them one, if I agreed to it."

"They're making them safer than before, Brett. Don't worry. At least, you'll know they're eating decent food and not scarfing down junk."

"You're right, sweetheart."

"The boys will be all right. At least, Josh is upstairs from them, keeping an eye on them. Are Marin and the gang coming for an extended visit soon?"

"I hope so. I'll get to spend more time with my precious little ladybug. I love her so much, I can't see straight."

"She's a beauty. Like her mother and grandmother."

"Poor Marin's still too thin. I'm worried about her."

"It's that Emerald. She's trying to drive that girl to developing that new disorder: Anorexia Nervosa."

"I've heard it can kill you. Isn't that how Karen Carpenter died? I'm so mad, I'm going over there to give that Emerald a piece of my mind! I've been biting my tongue to keep the peace, but no more."

"That woman is pure evil. Marin knows that. She's not going to let her manipulate her. You could just keep emphasizing to her that she shouldn't listen to Emerald."

"She is eating healthy. She's too sensible to let her get to her. I'll keep a close watch. Why are we standing out here? Why don't we go in and have some tea?"

Lea followed her into the house and closed the door behind them.

* * *

She planted feverish kisses on the child's cheeks. They looked, felt, and tasted like ripe nectarines. Her hands were plump and round like tea biscuits.

"Your Gram loves you very much; yes , she does; yes, she does."

She pressed her close to her heart. The child bit passionately on the plastic teething ring in her hand; her strawberry blonde curls broke loose from under her eyelet bonnet.

"Gram's going to see you again very soon." she kissed her cheeks again and handed her to Marin.

In her pink fleece pants with the purple flowers and her pink sweatshirt with kittens on it, she appeared toasty warm on this breezy afternoon. It could easily turn chilly on days like this, particularly after dusk. Sam buckled her into the infant's seat in the car and Marin pulled the bright purple blanket around her for additional warmth. A lime green stuffed elephant was beside her and she hugged him in delight. As Marin took her own seat, Sam placed the diaper bag and the gifts Brett had given them in the back seat.

"Bye, Ladybug, Cream Cupcake." Brett waved at Brettiella and blew kisses, "Gram loves you!"

"Take care of yourself, Mom. I love you." Marin called out.

"I love you, sweetheart. You take good care of yourself, too." she waved, "Have a safe trip back."

Brett stood watching until the car rounded the corner, oblivious to the lipstick imprints on her cheeks from Marin. She had locked her house and brought her keys in her jean pocket. It was a good, dry evening for planting bulbs, perhaps in front of her living room window. She unlocked the padlock on the garden shed behind Maggie's place, obscured from view by tall elms. Beyond the neglected clearing past the elms, an eight foot wooden fence separated the property from that of the grey house directly behind them.

A lumpy figure behind the forsythia bushes caught her eye. Red flannel moved in and out of view. Garden spade in hand, she proceeded toward the clearing.

"Who is it? Who's out there?" she called out, expecting a desperate thief.

No one answered. Red flannel behind the forsythia slithered towards the tall fence.

"Come out, whoever you are! I know you're there!" she called out again, stealthily approaching the clearing.

Then, she saw him: Grotesque, grimy, oily.

"What do you want?" she called out in a calm voice, though her heart was fluttering in her ribcage.

"You're leading a wanton life, Brett Morrow." a deep voice called back, "You must be punished for your sins."

"Mr. Pearson, go home. Your wife needs you." she pleaded, hoping thoughts of his invalid wife would return him to reality.

"You're a wicked woman." he continued approaching her, his doughy, lumpy form treading on the moist earth, bruising the grass.

"Please go home." she stepped back.

"You need to be taught a lesson."

"Don't come any closer." she held up her spade.

"A little slip of a thing like you don't scare me." he flashed crooked, brown teeth and laughed maniacally.

"I'll scream!"

"No one'll hear you over the traffic." he laughed again.

"Maggie will! My other neighbors will!"

"No one's home. Your Maggie went out with some old couple a while ago, and your next door neighbors are away in Prince Edward Island. Them people out back are out, too. So, you see, ain't no one around to hear you."

"Don't come any closer! I'm warning you!"

"You have to pay for your sins, Jezebel! You were sent here by Satan to tempt men with your evil ways. I see you comin' home, a different man on your arm every day, laughin', carryin' on. You shameless hussy! Wearin' them low-cut dresses, showin' your breasts! You'll burn in hell!"

"Please go away. I've never done anything to you."

"I'm gonna get me what I been missin'. Why should other men have all the pleasure? C'mere, my little chickadee." he took a brazen step toward her, slipping off the suspenders holding up his charcoal work pants.

She waved her spade threateningly in his direction, however, he snatched it out of her hand and flung it on the ground. He produced a fraying length of rope from his back pocket and tied her hands behind her. He shoved her into the garden shed and blocked the entrance with a wheelbarrow. Producing a soiled white handkerchief from the pocket of his red flannel shirt, he gagged her. His fingers ripped the front of her chambray blouse. With a sinister grin, he squeezed her breasts with such force that she thought she might lose consciousness. He threw her on the cold dirt floor as he dropped his baggy pants and white boxers. He came down upon her with his full leaden weight, unzipped her jeans and pulled them down around her ankles. In the corner of her eye, she could see shiny black beetles crawling beside her head.

"Don't fight me." his face loomed menacingly above hers, "Don't fight me, or I'll have to hurt you. I don't want to hurt you. You're so pretty." he lowered the gag and began kissing her fiercely.

It was the sloppy, malodorous, clumsy kissing of an inept man unfamiliar with women. His salty tongue searched the caverns of her mouth, savoring each spot. Deprived of oxygen, she was choking.

When he finally lifted his face from hers, he gagged her again and bit into her already tender breasts. His frenzied fingers then explored every inch of her flesh, pinching, squeezing...The stench of his unbathed, aging skin made her nauseous. He entered her with such great force, she felt her flesh ripping. His nostrils were flaring in delight, his eyes glowing with madness, perspiration trickling down his forehead, oozing out of every exposed pore as he panted like a wet Saint Bernard. Everything inside her was becoming toxic and foul. Her flesh was wasting away under his weight. He squealed like a pig. When he was done with her, he scrambled to his feet clumsily, fumbling with pockets and buttons. Kicking the wheelbarrow aside, he fled like a grizzly with a picnic basket. The shed door swung in the wind, squeaking rhythmically. Her thighs were slimy. She slithered on her back toward the door, her hands still tied beneath her, paralyzed from her own weight. She attempted to grunt loud enough to be heard over the gag. Her jeans were still around her ankles and her blouse ripped open. With every ounce of her strength, she managed to roll herself onto her stomach, thus only exposing her buttocks. The flattened carcass of a small garden beetle on the left cheek of her buttocks peeked out like a tattoo, framed by imprints of straw from the shed floor. Then, the tears came – a torrent, unabashed, unstoppable. She wept for what seemed to be an eternity before she heard a female voice above her head.

"My Goodness! Moe, get some help!"

"My dear, beautiful Brett! Who did this to you?" this was Maggie, "Connie, dear, take my key out of my pocketbook, go in and call an ambulance." she proceeded to remove Brett's gag and untie her hands; she pulled her jeans up to cover her as Moe, the stupefied white-haired man watched.

"The poor, poor thing." Connie searched for Maggie's key, "Come on, Moe, the poor woman doesn't need you gawking at her fanny!"

Reluctantly, he followed her into Maggie's apartment. Maggie removed her own pink cardigan and covered Brett's exposed breasts by putting it on her with the buttons in the back. Brett was able to turn herself around by leaning on Maggie, who gathered her in an embrace.

"Who did this to you, darling?"

"Abel Pearson." she sobbed, "He said I needed to be punished for my wicked ways."

"That maniac! He's not going to get away with this! He'll be put away."

"What's going to happen to his wife?"

"I reckon Social Services will have to step in and put her in the hospital until an opening comes up in a nursing home."

"Poor woman...Her only son's already in jail for selling drugs."

"The pear didn't fall far from the tree."

As the wailing of sirens approached, a single gunshot rang out down the street, shattering the quiet hum of children's games in the park. A single gunshot; clear and loud and unmistakable.

Chapter 20/ MIND GAMES

"You're home early, dear." Edna greeted her in the entryway.

"Queen Lea practically kicked me out." Sydney removed her coat and hung it on the coat tree.

"Kicked you out? How can she do that? It's not even her house."

"Well, Lea seems to think otherwise." Sydney removed her shoes and slipped into her ballerina flats.

"That's preposterous!" her dad called out from the living room.

Kissing Edna's cheek and wrapping one arm around her, she walked with her into the living room to embrace her dad.

"I'm sorry you've been put in this position, dealing with that dreadful woman, dear." he kissed her forehead.

"I wanted to comfort Brett and spend some time with her, but she wouldn't leave us alone for even a minute. She didn't even go to the bathroom to give us a chance to catch up. Brett asked her to give us time alone but she refused, saying she didn't want Brett to overexert herself. She seemed to think somehow it was her responsibility to look out for Brett's wellbeing."

"She's a very difficult woman."

"Then, she insisted Tony stay the night in the guest room, so he could spend more time with Aurelie. When he refused, she threatened to keep the baby away from him. She's playing so many mind games."

"You should not have to deal with this." her dad fumed, "I hope Tony put his foot down."

"He tried. But he was already feeling defeated after the showdown with his parents."

"He should've tried harder. He needs to put his foot down. You are his first priority. He cannot allow that woman to torment you like this."

"It's not his fault, Dad. He's worried about losing access to his daughter. He offered to drive me home, but I refused. I thought the walk would help me clear my head."

"But this is unacceptable. They can't treat my daughter like this!"

"Lea's turned it into a choice between me and his daughter. His hands are tied."

"And Old Willy and Mildred threatened to disown him if he marries you." Edna shook her head.

"I think maybe our relationship is doomed." Sydney sat on the sofa and buried her face in her hands. "Lea's trying to get him to rekindle his relationship with Brett, in order to keep both of them close to her and set up some sort of a domestic arrangement with them. She sees me as an interloper."

"She is the interloper." Sid shouted, "If Tony loves you as much as he says he does, he needs to step up and protect you."

"She's the mother of his child." she said.

"He can sue for full custody. He is a Horncastle."

"He wouldn't want to hurt her."

"But he doesn't mind hurting you?" his face was crimson.

"Sid, dear, please don't get all worked up." Edna pleaded.

"Yes, Dad, please don't worry." Sydney wound her arms around his neck, "I'm sure he'll find a way. Everything will work out."

"I'm watching him." he shook his index finger, "He'd better get his act together. I'm not going to allow anyone to hurt my daughter."

"I love you so much, Dad." she kissed his cheek, "I don't want to make you two late for your dinner."

"We can cancel it."

"Please don't do that. I want you to go out, have a nice meal, go to the Symphony concert, enjoy yourselves."

"Come with us."

"No. This is your night out. Besides, I'm too tired to enjoy a concert now. I just want to grab a quick bite, do some laundry, put my feet up and read a book."

"If you say so, dear."

"Yes I do. Come on, get ready, you two."

* * *

From the laundry room window, she studied the main house, silently majestic and forlorn with its blinds drawn even on this bright day. Weathered, cracked, greying white paint had worn down to bare wood in places, landing an air of neglect. This grand mansion guarding sinister truths concealed behind its aging plaster...Even in its shabby splendor, it stood as a testament to the opulence of

Beavertown's privileged class. In stark contrast, her parents' house hid in shame behind an overgrown hedge, with its matching aged white paint and austere mid-century style.

Charcoal clouds were dancing a menacing tango across the sky. She picked up the wicker basket and ran out to the wooden deck to gather her delicate garments from the clothesline.

Muffled voices were coming from the Horncastles' patio – at first, a low drone, then, raised to a crescendo.

"You know, Millie, dear, there are plenty of fascinating tidbits I could tell Tony about you and Brother Willy." this was Warren.

"There's absolutely nothing Tony doesn't know."

"Is that right? Now, let me see...He does know about you and Willy, back in '71, offering Brett thirty thou to leave Tony alone and Brett throwing you out of her house in absolute outrage...Sound familiar?"

"It's a lie! You can't believe a word that strumpet says!"

"I have it on very good authority that it is, indeed true. Now, you don't want me to tell Tony about all your dirty little secrets, do you?"

"Tony would never believe anything you have to say."

"I'm sure he'd be plenty interested in this. Of course, there's also that other matter regarding Guido..."

There was dead silence. Who was Guido, Sydney wondered, folding a blue nylon negligee. It was a name she did not remember having heard before.

"You...You..." Mildred raged, "They were right about you! You bite the hand that feeds you! Who was it that got you off when those trollops accused you of rape? How soon we forget. Willy worked night and day to get you that 'not guilty' verdict. This is the thanks he gets!"

"He did that to protect the family name."

"You ingrate! You repulse me!"

"Of course I do. That is my entire purpose in life: To repulse people. And, Tony's going to be plenty repulsed when he learns about what you and Willy have been up to."

"What's going on out here?" this was Willy.

"Millie and I are having a nice chat, aren't we, Sis, dear?"

"Willy, he's threatening to tell Tony…About the thirty thousand and about…you know…"

"Brother Willy and I know of yet another secret he wants kept under wraps, don't we, Brother?"

"Get out! Get out at once!"

"You'd better sit down, Willard, dear. You don't look too well. Would you like me to call Dr. Wagg?" Millie whined.

"I'll be fine. Mildred, dear, would you leave the two of us alone, please?"

"Don't get too riled up, dear. Remember your blood pressure."

"I'll be fine. I want a private word with my brother."

"Yes, dear."

The screen door squeaked as Mildred obeyed him.

"I want you to leave her alone! Leave all of us alone! This is inhuman. You're putting my wife through hell!"

"But it was all right for the two of you to put Tony, Brett and Dottie through hell, and now to put Sydney and her family through hell!"

"Those things happened a long time ago. Everyone's forgotten about them by now. If you insist on dredging it all up, you'll be hurting a lot of people."

"Yes. You and Millie. I think Tony deserves to know the truth. It might be painful initially for him to process it and accept what assholes his parents are, but he'll be far better off in the long run. The truth is always better in the long run."

"I want you to drop this, or...or..."

"Or what? You'll arrange for me to have an accident? You're an expert at that, aren't you, Brother? I think I'll take my chances. If anything happens to me, they'll know to come looking for you."

"Get out!"

"You are not going to stand in the way of Tony's happiness. He wants to marry Sydney and build a life with her. It's none of your business, so butt out!"

"She's a black widow. Look what happened to Jack."

"You need to look no further than our own dear sister Audrey for what happened to Jack."

"Get out! Get out now! Get out, or I'll call the police!"

"I'll leave. But, remember, Willy. Remember."

Sydney heard the slamming of a door and observed Warren crossing the lawn toward her.

"Hello, Stormy." he came up the wooden stairs to the deck, "I suppose you heard that kerfuffle."

"It was difficult not to."

"Looks like there's a storm brewing." he glanced up at the sky, "How fitting for a night like this. I'll bring in your laundry basket."

"Thank you." she held the door open for him.

"Looks like we're both outcasts now, Stormy. Both of us have been banished from the Horncastle Kingdom." he placed the basket in the hallway outside the den.

"Are you all right?"

"I'll be fine. That stuff slides right off my back." he sat on the loveseat. "Do you have anything to drink?"

"All we have is white wine, I'm afraid."

"It'll do."

In the distance, thunder roared and the sound of the wind knocking down and dragging away the wooden deck furniture jarred them both.

"I'll take care of that." he dashed outside.

She followed him, and the two of them gathered the red Adirondack chairs from the lawn. The downpour drenched them without mercy. He carried the chairs to the small unlocked shed behind the house and secured the door with a rock. He returned a soggy, dripping mess, reluctant to venture too far into the kitchen.

"Thank you, Warren. I'll put your clothes in the dryer." she said.

He pulled her into his arms and kissed her fiercely. She managed to squirm away.

"God, I want you! I still want you! I still can't get you out of my head!" he kissed her again.

"Warren, please don't do this." she pleaded. "Let me just put your wet clothes in the dryer. I'll get you a bathrobe."

She ran into the laundry room and returned with a white terry bathrobe. As she turned to leave, he called out to her.

"Where are you going, Stormy? Are you afraid the temptation would be too great for you if you stayed here? Would it drive you wild? You wouldn't be able to control yourself."

She heard the jingling of his belt buckle as his trousers hit the floor.

"Here they are." he said, prompting her to turn around to find him smirking, standing proudly in all his glory.

"Missed it, eh?" he winked.

"Put on the robe! Or you're out of here, clothes or no clothes!"

"You're cruel, Stormy. Can't you see I'm aching for you?"

"Warren, I mean it. Put on the robe. Or you're going home in my purple gypsy dress."

"It's not as if there's anything you haven't seen before." he complied reluctantly, "You really drive a hard bargain. Aren't you going to get out of your wet clothes?"

"Once your stuff's in the dryer." she took the pile of his clothes to the laundry room.

He heard the hum of the motor and tiptoed down the hall. He opened the door to the laundry room where she was undressing.

"No!" she stated firmly, "Get out of here!"

"Yes, ma'am." he saluted her and returned to the living room.

She appeared a short while later, dressed in a pale blue robe and proceeded to pour drinks.

"Warren," she frowned, "Who's Guido?"

"No one." he snapped and rose suddenly, "I have to go. I'll get my clothes from the dryer."

"They're not ready yet."

"I'll wear them as they are. I don't have too far to walk, anyway."

"If you want to go home, just dash across the lawn quickly in the robe. You can pick up your clothes in the morning. I'll have them ready for you."

"Thanks, Stormy. I mean that. Thanks for everything."

"You're welcome. Thanks for taking care of the chairs."

"Hang in there, Stormy." he patted her shoulder, "See you later."

Chapter 21/ SECRETS

Warren locked his door and settled in his black leather chair behind his heavy walnut desk. He tore open the manila envelope in his hand and spread out the photographs across the desk. He picked them up one by one and analyzed them in detail.

"Well, well, well..." he laughed under his breath, "Let's see what you've been up to, you duplicitous broad."

He gathered up the images of the brunette engaged in heated interaction outside a garage with a scruffy man in blue coveralls and placed them back in the envelope.

"You've been a naughty girl." he rose and removed a dismal landscape from the wall; he placed it on the floor against the wall. "You're not as clever as you think you are."

He opened the combination wall safe, deposited the envelope and closed it again. He rotated the barrel and hung up the painting in its place.

"I'd like to know what you and this Bruiser guy are up to." he sat back at his desk and plugged in a cassette tape recorder.

He attached a set of headphones to the machine. Retrieving a key from a flowerpot on the windowsill, he unlocked the right top drawer of the desk and produced a cassette. He inserted it into the machine and put on the headphones.

"There's something wrong with the baby." the first voice stated, "The doctor said they need to do additional tests, but he's quite certain it's something called Segawa Disease."

In the background, muffled voices, footsteps, and the sound of dishes against one another could be heard.

"I'm so sorry, hon. I'm afraid I've been so preoccupied with my own stuff that I missed all the warning signs."

"You had a lot on your plate. I told him about how rigid her arms and legs are, how she has those jerky movements. She's not developing properly for a six month old baby. After a round of tests, he said it was Segawa Disease. It's a rare genetic disorder."

"I'm so sorry, hon."

"You know how we both noticed earlier that she had no facial expression...Well, that was one of the indicators...We'll have to go to Halifax to see more specialists...I hope Tony can come with us. I could really use his support at a time like this."

"I'm sure he'll go, sweetheart. She's his top priority; you know that. We'll tell him about this together."

"If you're done with your coffee, why don't we get out of here? I don't like that creepy guy at the next booth behind you. He's got his nose in his newspaper, but keeps looking up to stare at me."

"Maybe he's checking you out. He thinks you're a babe."

"Don't turn around. Wait till we get up; take a look on the way out."

The recording ended there. Warren burst into laughter.

"Well, Elliott, old pal, you always come through for me."

He removed the cassette, placed it in its clear plastic protective case and returned it to the drawer, locking it afterwards. He leaned back in his chair, smiling broadly.

* * *

"Both of you are all smiles." Edna greeted them, "What's happened to cause this good mood?"

"We're coming back from Watkinson's Jewellers." Tony announced.

"That's where marriage licences are issued." Sid stated solemnly.

"Yes, Dad." Sydney beamed, "We have our licence and we've set the date."

"This is kind of sudden, isn't it?" her dad frowned.

"We don't want to wait any longer." Tony said.

"When is the date?" Edna asked.

"Next Tuesday. In the Justice Building."

"That gives us only five days to prepare." Edna said.

"There's no need for any preparations." Sydney said, "All we need are two witnesses and the two of you."

"Have you chosen the witnesses yet?"

"Yes. Dottie and J.T. After all, they're newlyweds, too, and they also bucked tradition by eloping."

"My beautiful daughter. I'm so happy for you!" Edna embraced her and shook Tony's hand.

"Dad?" she tentatively approached him.

"Congratulations." he said, "I hope you're sure this is what you want."

"It is, Dad." she murmured with tearful eyes.

"I hope this fellow makes you happy." he glanced suspiciously at Tony, "You and I need to have a little chat, son."

"Yes sir."

"I know you're a proud father and all that, but I need some reassurance that you are willing to do anything necessary to protect my daughter from the mother of your child. I am not pleased with the way things have been. I want you to put my daughter first."

"Sydney is, and has always been my first priority, sir. I love her more than life itself and there's nothing I wouldn't do for her."

"Then, show it."

"I promise."

"Remember, young man: I'll be watching you. If you make her cry, you'll answer to me."

"Yes sir."

Sydney longed to tell her father that Tony had cut ties with his parents to marry her.

"Let's celebrate." Edna proposed, "I'll get some Club Soda for us, and you can have some white wine we keep on hand for guests."

"No, we'll have Club Soda, as well." Tony said, tightening the arm he had around Sydney.

"In all the excitement, I forgot to ask if you have the rings yet." Edna said.

"We do." Sydney held out her left hand to showcase a dazzling diamond solitaire, "Tony had it custom made for me."

"It's beautiful."

"Thank you."

"Come on; come here." Sid motioned to her, tears streaming down his cheeks.

"I love you, Dad." she wound her arms around his neck and kissed his cheek.

"I love you, sweetheart." he squeezed her hand.

* * *

"What's all the commotion?" Warren appeared in the atrium to find Lea engaged in a lively dispute with Maxine.

"She won't let me see Tony!" Lea shouted, "She says he's out of town. I know she's lying!"

"I'll handle this, Maxine." he said, "I apologize for Mademoiselle's behavior."

"Yes sir." Maxine returned to the kitchen.

"What is it with you, Lea?" he barked, "You've been told he's out of town. Why do you keep making a nuisance of yourself and abusing our staff?"

"You're all trying to keep me away from him, but I know my rights. I'm the mother of his child. I have every right to see him whenever I want. It's an urgent matter. It's a medical problem with our baby."

"Well, he's out of town and you can't see him now."

""I don't believe you. Where is he? He didn't mention any business trips."

"He's on his honeymoon." he smiled deliciously.

And, a pale Lea collapsed with great noise on the Art Deco ceramic floor.

Chapter 22/ SERENDIPITY

His back to the door, slouched over the table, he savored his Minestrone soup in solitude. With every customer who walked in, a gust of wind sent a chill through him. His duffle coat was no match for this bitter November wind.

"Here's your dessert, Johnny." the middle-aged waiter placed a plate of apple pie a la mode on his table. "Your usual."

"Thanks, Al." he smiled.

"You're like clockwork, Johnny." the man said. "You come here after you get off work; you order Minestrone soup, Sprite, and apple pie a la mode."

"I guess I'm a creature of habit, Al."

"Maybe, one of these days, I can coax you into trying something else." he turned to wait on the other customers.

The door opened and a couple strolled in, hands linked and giddy with love. They appeared over-dressed for this greasy spoon. It was not that out of the ordinary to find the occasional customers coming in after taking in a play nearby to catch a bite of sinful fried delicacies dressed in their Sunday best. They took a booth across the aisle, three rows back. Al approached them promptly.

"We'd like two cheeseburger platters, please." the man said.

"What would you like to drink?"

"Two Sprites, please."

"Coming right up."

Once alone, the couple linked hands across the table and whispered with bowed heads. Then, the man rose, approached the woman and helped her remove her black fur coat before removing his own long black wool coat. Comfortably settled, they linked hands once again. Their voices were too hushed to be heard. He wondered why the woman seemed so eerily familiar. Her glistening dark hair was in a bob. She was dressed in a sumptuous green velvet dress, displaying bare arms and tantalizing cleavage. His heart skipped a beat. He shifted his position in discomfort.

"Happy birthday to my beautiful wife and soulmate." the man spoke up, producing a small gift-wrapped box from his breast pocket.

"Oh, Tony..." she opened it and produced a diamond necklace. "Sweetheart, thank you so much!"

"I want you to know how much I love you."

"You know I don't need any lavish gifts. I only care about being with you."

He went over to her side of the booth to put it on her.

"You are the most beautiful woman in the world. You should be surrounded by beautiful things."

"All I need is you."

He bent down to kiss her.

"Hey, you two, get a room!" a young man from a nearby booth shouted.

He observed Al serving their humble meal. How incongruous for this affluent couple to be having a cheeseburger platter at a greasy spoon, instead of dining in a posh restaurant, he mused.

"I'm the luckiest man on earth to be married to a woman like you, Sydney Horncastle." the man said.

Sydney...Sydney...It was her...Tears welled up in his eyes. He bolted like a wounded stallion and ran into the night.

"Hey, Johnny!" Al called out after him, "Johnny, where's the fire? You didn't pay for your meal!"

"We'll pay for his meal." Tony intercepted, approaching the cash register. "He must've remembered something he had to do or some place he needed to be."

"This is the first time he's pulled anything like this. Johnny's usually a pretty dependable fellow. It's not a big deal, anyhow. I know where to find him." he took Tony's credit card to process it. "He sings at the gay club around the corner. Johnny Cantrell is his name. A sad fellow."

"He must be lonely." Sydney mused, "I hope he finds some happiness soon."

* * *

The street lights and the headlights from the cars blended into a watercolor painting left out in the rain. The stream of his tears blurred all before him as he ran blindly through the streets. Oblivious to the car horns cautioning him and drivers shouting profanities at him, he kept running. He did not know whether Stephen would be home now. Lately, it had become difficult to communicate with him. He was disappearing at all hours, not returning home for days at a time. When he reached their building, he opened the security door with his key and took the elevator to the fifth floor, instead of their floor. He knocked tentatively on an apartment door.

"Who is it?"

"It's me, Jack, Aydin."

The door was promptly opened and he was ushered inside.

"You look terrible, man. Come in. I'll get you a drink." Aydin led him into the living room. Kent immediately hugged him.

"I'm sorry about the late hour."

"No problem." Aydin poured him a scotch.

"I couldn't go up to the empty apartment. Stephen is never there. Even when he's there, we don't talk much anymore."

"Well, you came to the right place." Kent sat beside him. "Obviously, something's happened to get you in this state."

"I saw her."

"Her...Sydney?"

"Yes, Sydney."

"Here in New York?"

"Yes. She's remarried."

"That was quick."

"She's a beautiful woman. I'm not surprised. Her new husband is loaded. He gave her a diamond necklace for her birthday."

"Where did you see them? At the club?"

"No. At Al's."

Both laughed.

"They must've seen a play, and decided to experience a down home ambience." Jack said.

"You've got it bad, man." Aydin said. "You don't remember anything about your past, but you remember her name and her face. You still feel the love you felt for her."

"She's moved on. She looked very happy with this new man. I'm happy for her."

"But it cuts like a knife, doesn't it?" Kent said. "Maybe you need to go back home, buddy. Come clean. Tell her the whole sordid story about your memory loss. Tell her how much you still love her."

"I can't do that to her. I can't mess up her life. This chap makes her happy. She deserves so much better than me."

"Jack, Jack, Jack." Aydin sat on the other side of him and placed an arm around him. "You need to reclaim your life."

"This is my life now, guys. I belong with Stephen."

"I think it's about time you found out the truth, Jack." Kent said, "Both of us have been tormented keeping this from you, but you need to know."

"What truth?"

"Stephen has not been truthful with you, Jack. The two of you never had a relationship in the past. You are not bisexual. You've never been attracted to men."

Jack was speechless.

"Yes. Sydney was the love of your life. But your family set up a scheme to tear you apart. Unfortunately, it worked."

"And she moved on. But it's not too late to claim what's yours. Go back to her, Jack."

"She loves this new guy now."

"I wonder who he is."

"She called him Tony. Good looking guy. The last name was Horncastle."

"Oh, my God!" Aydin exclaimed. "I don't believe it!"

"Why? Do you know him?"

"He's your cousin, best friend, and former business partner." Kent explained.

"And obviously an opportunist." Aydin added. "Now, you have to go back! You can't let him steal her away like this!"

"I can't."

"Don't make any decisions tonight." Kent suggested. "Stay here for the night and get some rest. You can face tomorrow with a clearer head and formulate your plan."

Chapter 23/ DECEPTION

Tony hung up the phone and hastily put on his pants.

"I'll have to go back." he said.

"Is something wrong?" Sydney sat up in bed.

"They're doing more tests. Apparently, Lea and Brett went to Halifax last week for some additional testing on Aurelie. Warren says I need to be tested, too. Something's up, obviously. He's going to fill me in when I get there." he put on his socks.

"I hope it goes well."

"They've already diagnosed her with Segawa Disease. It's caused by an inherited defective gene from either one of the parents. Warren says I need to be tested to see if she inherited it from me." he buttoned his shirt.

"Has Lea been tested and ruled out?"

"I don't really know. I don't even think the parents are routinely tested. There's no need. They already have the diagnosis and the treatment." he fastened his tie in front of the mirror.

"But Warren insists you get tested?"

"He must suspect something is amiss." he went into the adjoining bathroom and left the door open. "He's bought my ticket over the phone. It must be urgent."

"I'm going to take a later flight to join you."

"Are you sure you don't want to stay in Toronto? My parents are on the warpath."

"It's all right. I'll stay with my parents and out of their way. I want to be there for you through this ordeal."

"Warren's also cautioned us about not divulging any information to Brett. Unfortunately, she's in Lea's pocket and tells her everything."

"I understand."

"Now that Dottie and J.T. have moved into Jack's old suite, it's going to feel more like home. Warren and I felt like we were in enemy territory." he emerged from the bathroom with his hair gelled into place.

"I'll check us out and settle the bill." she said, wrapping a lacy pink robe around her.

"Thank you, sweetheart." he kissed her, "I appreciate your support. I love you."

"I love you. See you tonight."

"Call me when you land. I'll come and get you."

"Never mind. You're going to be busy. I'll take a cab."
"Have a safe flight."

"You, too, sweetheart." she kissed him.

No one was going to intimidate her into hiding out in Toronto any longer. She was a Horncastle now and she planned to take her rightful place by Tony's side.

* * *

"Warren persuaded the doctor to convince Lea to be tested. I don't know what he said to her, but she went along with it. And, the results are in." Tony took both of her hands

223

in his, "Neither one of us is the carrier for the defective gene."

"That means..."

"Yes. Aurelie is not mine. She inherited the gene from her real father, whoever the poor sucker might be."

"Wow." she shook her head in disbelief, "She carried on quite the charade there, didn't she? Now, what happens?"

"She's been sent packing back to her parents' place in Bathurst."

"She needs to return the child support she extorted from you all this time."

"That's all right. None of this is Aurelie's fault."

"Anyone have any information about who the real father might be?"

"Warren's detective narrowed it down to a mechanic named Bruiser from the North Side. He observed Lea visiting him quite frequently. They were apparently conspiring to extort a great deal of money from us."

"She fooled everyone into believing she was this old-fashioned girl next door."

"At one time, she was that sweet girl next door. I realize now I must have hurt her badly when I had a casual fling with her years ago. She wanted revenge for the shabby way I treated her."

"As a woman, I can relate to feeling enraged for being used, but I can't understand taking it to this level."

"She must really hate me. When I think back to the time she showed up out of the blue and initiated sex, I realize now their plan was already in action and she was already pregnant. I was such an idiot."

"She must've been very bitter to commit such a heinous act. You believed all those months Aurelie was yours and bonded with that little girl. This is cruel beyond words."

"Good thing Warren was on top of things. She would have gotten away with this deception had it not been for his suspicious mind."

"She fooled all of us. Brett opened her home to her. Her kids bonded with her."

"Her obsession with Brett was always a puzzle."

"Brett must be devastated. I'll go visit her tomorrow."

"We need to come up with a new name for the club now."

"How about Tony's?"

"I have a better idea: Sydney's."

"You'd go out of business in one day. You'd better stick with Tony's."

"That sounds so conceited."

"Then, how about Dorothy's?"

"I love that! Thank you." he embraced her, "Everything's starting to look up. I don't know where I'd be now if you hadn't come into my life."

* * *

Kent found the note on the kitchen counter beside the coffee maker.

"Dear Kent and Aydin,

Thank you for putting me up for the night and for opening my eyes. I have decided to leave New York and start over somewhere else, but not Beavertown. I can't go back to resume my old life. There's been too much water under the bridge. Again, thank you for being true friends. I'll be in touch once I have a place to call home. Take care. My regards, Jack"

Chapter 24/ SACRIFICE

"I want you to pack your bags and get out of our house!" Mildred cornered Sydney in the sunroom. "I don't want my son with the likes of you. You're going to divorce him and forfeit any kind of financial gain from this misguided union."

"I don't want your money." she said wearily.

"You're going to tell him you realized you don't love him and you want your freedom. You're going to leave town and never contact my son. You'll receive no settlement and no alimony."

"I never wanted anything from you. But I am not going to hurt Tony to appease you. I think he has a right to know what you're doing behind his back."

"You will not breathe a word to him, do you hear me?"

"And what if I do?"

"You don't want to find out."

"I'm willing to sign anything to get the lot of you off my back, but I'm not going to keep this from Tony. I want what's in his best interest and I'll do everything to protect him."

"We'll just see about that."

"This family eats its young. What Audrey's done to Jack and what you're doing to Tony are heinous. I wish I could've protected Jack, but at least, I can protect Tony."

"You're going to eat those words, Missy. You'll be very sorry you ever messed with us." Mildred shook an index finger in her face and stormed out of the room.

* * *

Brett, Chuck, Gene and Johnny O. greeted them at the door. Brett kissed them both on the cheek and the men shook their hands. Tony was beaming, his eyes taking in every detail of the fresh interior. The scent of paint bleeding through the overpowering sweet scent of fresh flowers made Sydney nauseous. She blinked away her tears. Jack should be here for this momentous occasion. The club was a magnificent sight to behold in Streamline Moderne style. Brett kept an arm around her as Tony conducted a final inspection before opening the club for customers. She hid in the staff lavatory until the crowds arrived to admire this dazzling jewel in the urban core.

"Ladies and gentlemen," Tony stepped on the platform which had replaced the stage and motioned to Sydney to join him. "My lovely wife Sydney and I welcome you to the grand re-opening of our club, now named 'Dorothy's'. A brand new building, a brand new name, a brand new vibe. There will be some changes, but rest assured, we're always going to remain your old favorite jazz club. We're going to be featuring up and coming jazz musicians on Friday nights. We have our regular singers Sydney Horncastle and Brett Morrow back, and we have hired a new singer, Dustin Flowers." Tony was the most animated she had seen him in a very long time. "And, all of your favorite faces are back: Johnny O'Hara, our Maître' D, Charles Seabrook, our accompanist, and our house band Gene And The Matchmakers. We hope you'll enjoy tonight's entertainment. We're featuring 'Hungry Crows', a fresh new band and our new vocalist, Dustin. All drinks are half price from eight to ten. Thank you for your support." he took her hand and led her away.

Gene And The Matchmakers began to play "Love's Theme", the disco anthem from the previous decade.

She remembered standing here with Jack on that fateful night...singing "Our Love Is Here To Stay" before their world crashed. What right did she have to be back here now, standing beside Tony? Jack should be here tonight, not her. This was Jack and Tony's club. If only she could have died that night, Jack would never have been spirited away. He would be celebrating the re-opening of his and Tony's new club. Jack would have marveled at this architectural masterpiece. If only he could have seen the expertly crafted curved corners, the glass bricks and portholes. If he would only walk through that door now, she would sign her half of the business to him on the spot and walk out of all their lives. Perhaps, then, Tony and Brett would finally have the happiness that had been denied to them. And, Jack would have his life back. Things would go back to the way they had been before she had stained their lives. She had never belonged here.

"Sweetheart, are you all right?" Brett nudged her.

"I thought I could handle it, but..."

"Flashbacks?"

She nodded.

Brett pulled her close and kept her arm around her.

Perhaps, Jack would return if he were certain she would not be here. After all, when contacted by Tony's associates, he had not contested the divorce. He had not fought to keep her. Letting her go had not been a struggle. Her absence would set things right for everyone: Brett and Tony, Jack and his Stephen.

"Yo, Brett." Chuck motioned to Brett, "We need your expertise back here."

Patting her on the back, Brett followed Chuck.

"Well, I see you've made yourself at home here again." a familiar voice was behind her.

"Celia." Sydney acknowledged her coldly.

"You don't let the grass grow under your feet, do you, Sydney? You go from one man to another in record time. What are you trying to prove?"

Without a word, Sydney walked away from her and slipped outside. The sky was clear and the stars were accommodating on this mild November night. Music and laughter from the club spilled out to The Green. They were playing "Summertime". She walked along the river's edge.

"Jack! Jack!" she shouted out, sobbing uncontrollably, "Jack...Jack."

She collapsed on a park bench, trembling and repeatedly calling his name. Back at the club, the music played on.

Chapter 25/ SINS OF THE FATHER

Storm clouds were gathering overhead. The river was the color of tarnished silver. It was uncharacteristically mild for mid-December. She buttoned her trench coat and quickened her steps.

"I had a feeling you might be here." she heard him behind her.

"I thought it was best to leave you and your family alone to sort things out."

"It was a pretty ugly scene. I'm glad you didn't have to witness it."

"I'm sorry."

His eyes strangely lambent, he pulled her to himself and kissed her urgently. Raindrops fell on their faces and rested on her eyelashes. He released her gently and took her hand. She walked in silence beside him. Noticing her struggling in her heels, he guided her across The Green with his hand on her elbow.

Maxine opened the door as if on cue and took their coats. Sensitive to their pensive mood, she did not speak. Tony led her upstairs to their suite and pulled her close. Tears were glistening in his dark eyes.

"Sydney...My beautiful Sydney...My dearest love." he kissed her hair, "I never want to let you go."

"I never want you to let me go, Tony. I feel so blessed to have found you."

"If you could only know how much I love you...I want you to bask in the glow of being treasured."

"I love you, too, Tony."

"I hope, some day, I can become someone who is deserving of you."

"Tony, why are you talking like this? You're scaring me."

"I'm feeling so much shame and anger and disgust for my family right now. I don't know if I can ever come to terms with what I learned tonight."

"You know I'll do anything I can to get you through this."

"I know." he lifted her hands to his lips and kissed them. "This is so horrific. I feel so contaminated, so vile...I feel too ashamed to even touch you."

"Tony, you're nothing like your family. You're a kind, compassionate, honorable man. I feel honored to be with you."

"You're much too good for me. I can't shake off the Horncastle curse until I do some soul searching and emerge a better human being...serve mankind...make a difference...without a thought about personal gain. I need to cleanse myself. I can't be good enough for you until I am good enough for me."

Sydney felt a chill. She buried her face in his chest.

"I'm too ashamed to even speak of it." he caressed her hair.

"Please let me share your burden." she pleaded.

"You're too immaculate to even hear about such things."

"Tony, please." she held his hands in hers.

The bitter wail of sirens sent a chill down her spine. She ran to the window, opened the drapes and craned her neck as they came nearer.

"Don't worry." he reassured her, "They're probably on their way to Skyline Acres or Lincoln Heights."

Then, an ambulance came within view and turned into the Horncastles' circular driveway. Glancing over her shoulder, Tony bolted and ran out of the room. Sydney followed him. From the stairs, they could see the paramedics rushing into Willy's main floor den with a stretcher.

"What's happened?" an ashen Tony ran down the last few steps.

"It's your dad, Tony, dear." Annette told him.

He froze. Standing behind him, Sydney instinctively reached for his hand and squeezed it. After what seemed like an eternity, the paramedics swept past them with a chalky Willard on the stretcher.

"Dad!" Tony ran to his side.

Mildred was trailing behind, wringing her hands and whimpering like a lost puppy.

"This is all your fault!" she glared at her son with eyes of blue ice, "Yours and Warren's! You are no son of mine! Stay away from us! Don't you dare come to the hospital! You are no longer a Horncastle!"

Without affording him the opportunity to respond, she brushed past him and boarded the ambulance.

Sydney caught a glimpse of Warren in the background, and he met her gaze. Dottie emerged, pale and dishevelled.

"Why don't you and Dottie come with us, Tony?" Annette suggested as Donald rushed out to bring the car around.

"I'll drive Tony, Sydney and Dottie." Warren volunteered.

"I don't think it would be wise for you to show up at the hospital, Warren." Annette said, "The same goes for you, too, Sydney."

"Don't you think you'd better get a move on, then, sister-in-law? Millie needs you by her side." Warren smirked.

"I'm warning you: Don't entertain any thoughts of showing your face around that hospital." Annette shook an index finger at him.

"Don't worry. I'll be a good boy." he waited for her to leave as Donald pulled up, "Let's go."

Tony, Sydney, and Dottie followed him to his black Bentley. Dottie sat up front with Warren. Sydney held Tony's hand during the painfully long, silent ride to the hospital.

"He was arguing with me when it happened." Warren informed them as they pulled into the hospital parking lot.

"He was arguing with me not long before that." Tony said.

"You go on up and see them." Warren said, "I'll hang out in the cafeteria and ogle the nurses."

"They're going to be upset to see me, too." Sydney said, giving Tony a kiss on the cheek, "Maybe I'd better wait down here, too. Dottie, please take good care of Tony."

"Don't worry." Dottie led Tony to the elevator.

Sydney joined Warren in the cafeteria where he was waiting in line.

"Is J.T. working tonight?" she asked him.

"Yes, he is. It's going to be a long night." he said, "I'll get us some coffee. Why don't you choose a table?"

She complied and chose a table with a view of the elevators.

"Just the way you like it: Black and bitter." he returned with two cups and placed one in front of her.

"Warren, what is going on with Tony's parents? It may be none of my business, but I don't like the way it's affecting Tony."

"I let Tony in on a few secrets his old man had been keeping from him."

"He couldn't even talk about it. I didn't press it, but I would like to support him."

"Donald and Annette think I exposed Willy out of spite, but it wasn't like that. I didn't have a choice. I explained that to Tony."

"I have no doubt you had a good reason to expose them at this time, after obviously keeping it quiet for a long time."

"I kept it to myself all those years because, at that time, the truth would have caused more pain than the lies."

"What changed?"

"Someone I care about very much was in danger from them. Exposing them was the only way to stop them. They forced my hand. I didn't want Tony to be hurt this way, but, had I not done this, he would have been hurt much more."

"I don't think any of them care who gets hurt."

"You've got that right. I have to be honest with you, Stormy: I don't know what the fallout from this is going to be. I just want you to know that, no matter what happens, I never intended for this to hurt you or Tony in any way."

"I know that, Warren."

In the hallway, the elevator door opened and Dottie stepped out. She approached them robotically and wearily announced:

"He's dead."

Chapter 26/ MY SON MY SON

Dottie tapped on the door and called out softly.

"Sydney, it's me. Can I come in?"

"Of course, sweetheart." she opened the door.

"How are you holding up?" Dottie closed the door behind them.

"Hanging in there." Sydney zipped up a full suitcase and placed it beside three other full upright ones.

"Is there anything I can do to help?"

"I'm all done. Good thing a lot of my stuff was still at my parents'. Most of this stuff is Tony's. We're temporarily moving in with my parents."

"That's a good idea." Dottie sat on a leather club chair by the window.

"I'm arranging for my parents to move to Toronto." Sydney took the other club chair. "Mildred is a loose cannon. There's no telling what she might do next."

"It's good to get them away from this cesspool."

"My aunt and uncle's house is wheelchair accessible. They were renting the main floor unit to an older couple, who recently moved out, to live in a seniors' apartment. It's been cleaned and fixed up and sitting empty since then. There's an elevator between floors, anyway. My parents had no trouble with accessibility when they visited, even when the tenants lived there. The elevator goes from the back extension to the second floor. That area was locked, so the

237

tenants couldn't access it, but now, it's going to be one full, open family living area."

"I love big brick houses like theirs. There must be plenty of room for Aunt Edna and Uncle Sid's treasures, too."

"There is. And, they already know quite a few people from the Jewish community there. And, Dad is selling the store to Leonard Greene."

"It's the end of an era."

"Tony wants to sell the club, too. He wants to cut all ties to the family and the life he's led. I can't say I blame him."

"I can't blame him, either. What about you guys? Do you know what you're going to be doing?"

"It all depends on how Tony feels. I'll accept whatever he wants."

"Sydney, you're a saint."

"Hardly." she laughed, "I love him and want to do what's right for him."

"He's pretty shaken up, but, Warren had no choice."

"I remember Warren said he did it to prevent someone from being harmed."

"You." Dottie said, "That someone was you."

Sydney's mouth fell open.

"Uncle Willy put a hit out on you." Dottie stated.

Sydney was speechless.

"Warren has his team of spies and detectives: That's how he found out. That's also how he uncovered Lea's deception. That's also how he uncovered Linda's diabolical plan. When he found out you were in danger, he knew he had to act fast... Sydney, are you okay? Do you need some water? You look terrible."

"I'm okay, Dottie. Please tell me more."

"Uncle Willy was a monster. I'm glad he's dead. I hope he rots in hell."

"He's hurt all of us terribly."

"He murdered Tony's real dad."

Sydney's eyes grew as large as a doe's.

"Yes, it's true. He wasn't his real dad. Aunt Mildred had an affair with Guido, the chauffeur. Tony's his son. When Uncle Willy found out, he had Guido killed...Sydney, are you sure you're okay?"

"Now, I understand some things Tony was saying...Now I understand why he couldn't even speak of it."

"After Uncle Willy died, when my parents and Aunt Mildred were cleaning out his desk, they found some letters from an 'Alice Johnson'."

"Who is Alice Johnson?"

"Nobody knew. They thought she was a secret lover. So, they opened them up and read them. Are you sure you're ready to hear this?"

"Please go on."

"Alice Johnson was Aunt Audrey. Uncle Willy was helping her hide Jack. He made all the arrangements to switch him with that homeless man..."

"And killed that poor man..."

"Yes, and to have Jack airlifted to a hospital in Boston, where a deranged psychiatrist named Hollis Mazot conducted some bizarre brainwashing experiments on him, and gave him illegal drugs, which caused an irreversible memory loss...almost like some sort of chemical lobotomy...Aunt Audrey and this shrink have been on the lam for a long time, but her latest letter to Uncle Willy had her most recent post office box number in New Mexico. When Warren got wind of it, he reported it and they were able to track them down."

"This gets more and more deranged."

"They showed her on the news. She says she's done nothing wrong, and it was all for her son's sake, to keep him safe from imminent danger. She claims she had no idea Mazot's techniques were illegal."

"Unbelievable."

"Mazot's cooked. She's being extradited here. I thought you should know."

"Does this mean...Jack doesn't have his memory back?"

"Yes, it does. The unorthodox procedures and illegal drugs Mazot used on him cause irreparable brain damage. It would take nothing short of a miracle for him to remember anything at all."

"What about that news bulletin about him being an item with that Stephen guy?"

"That was most likely Stephen's deception, nothing more. I never liked that guy."

Sydney sprang to her feet and rushed into the adjoining bathroom. She turned on the tap and lifted the toilet seat. Sinking to her knees, she retched until she felt empty. Completely empty. She sat up, pulled her knees up to her chin and sobbed, the salty taste of her tears burning her tongue.

* * *

Aydin anxiously tore open the envelope and read the contents aloud to Kent:

"Dear Aydin and Kent,

Hope you guys are doing well. Sorry for the delay in my reply. I'm finally settled now in Idaho, working as a farmhand. Lots of clean, fresh air, wholesome food, and a roof over my head. I've even got a girl, Ellie. She's a waitress at the local diner. I'm buying her a promise ring for Valentine's Day. I'm afraid I have to use another alias, to keep my past from catching up to me: Johnny Parker. Hope you have a good Valentine's Day. Please keep in touch. Warm regards, Jack."

* * *

"Come on, Mil; let's go to the golf club for lunch." Annette sat beside Mildred on the sofa and patted her knee.

"I can't face all the people...I feel so humiliated..." she dried her eyes with a tissue.

"People don't know anything other than what Audrey's done."

"I don't want to see anyone. I can't deal with all their prying and poking...Annette, dear, I want my son back."

"You're the one who told him he was no longer welcome here."

"I miss him. I just want him to leave that dreaded woman and come back home."

"He's made his feelings very clear, Mil, dear. He wants nothing to do with any of us."

"It's all her fault. She's been nothing but a scourge. She's destroyed us all. Warren lost his job, had his name dragged through the mud; Jack's brain damaged; my Willy's gone; Audrey's a convicted felon; Tony's heartbroken...Why did she have to come to Beavertown? Why couldn't she stay lost and live out the rest of her miserable life in Montreal?"

"And, to think Donald helped look for her all those years ago."

"Your sister really gave birth to a devil-spawn, Annette, dear."

"I have to agree with you, Mil. There's been an ill wind blowing since she came to town. Sydney turned out to be such a destructive woman."

"I hope my Tony comes to his senses and gets away from her. I miss my son. I miss the way things used to be before that she-devil darkened our doorstep."

"So do I. Because of her, I haven't spoken to my sister for years. Now, she's moved away and any chance of reconciliation is gone."

"We've got each other, Annette, dear. She can't do anything to come between us."

"Of course. You and I are always going to stick to each other like glue." Annette patted her back, "Now, I insist you come out to lunch with me. We'll go anywhere you choose."

"We can't let her get us down." Mildred perked up, "I'll go up and get dressed. Why don't you help me choose a dress, dear?"

"I'd love to."

242

They scampered up the stairs like two schoolgirls with a devious secret.

Chapter 27/ NEVER LET ME GO

Laughter was spilling from the Horncastles' patio. She had been aware of the tantalizing aroma of barbecued steaks earlier in the evening. Now it was cocktails el fresco and big band music compliments of The Matthews Band. Pagoda lights in carnival colors were strung across the patio. They had impressive visitors: Senators, former Governor Generals, Prime Ministers, judges, members of parliament, deans, and professors. The Horncastles entertained in grand style. At one time, her parents would have been invited to these affairs. She spied Annette in a sequined red gown, laughing in wild abandon. Oblivious to the pain of others, enamored with herself, and lapping up the attention: That was her dear Aunt Annette. How could any woman sell her soul to revel in the wealth and power of that lifestyle and still be able to look herself in the mirror each day? How could a woman enslave herself to social convention and mindless conformity in exchange for comfort and security? The cost of social acceptance was too high – one she would never be willing to pay.

Behind her, Tony was sleeping peacefully through the noise. He often roamed the house at nights, alone with his impenetrable dark thoughts. She did not press him to speak. He had completed legal name change documents for both of them to eradicate all traces of the Horncastle legacy. He had adopted Guido's surname Rossi, and Anthony had become Antonio. He had also changed her surname back from Horncastle to Goldstein. He had sold the club to Leonard Greene and closed his law practice. Leonard had kept Brett, Chuck and Gene, as well as Dustin. He had asked her to stay, as well, however, she had declined. Warren had managed to track down Guido's impoverished relatives in a small village in Italy and Tony had wired them a generous sum.

Overcome by a sense of impending doom, she watched him closely, attempting to achieve a delicate balance without smothering him. There was an urgency in all he undertook, even in the way he made love to her. He was more forceful; he took a longer time to heighten her sensation. He wanted to experiment more, to maximize her pleasure. And, he did not allow her to pleasure him; he wanted it to be all about her.

"We're going to be all right." she had kissed his chest that afternoon, lying in his arms, "We're going to have a happy life somewhere, away from here. As long as we have each other, we'll find our way."

He had kissed her forehead and pulled her closer, his eyes dark and distant. Now, he was asleep at last, his brow still furrowed and tracks of dried tears still on his cheeks. Now unseen by him, she allowed her own tears to flow in an unabashed waterfall.

Laughter from the party was growing louder as the guests became more inebriated. A clearly tipsy Mildred wove through the tables, hanging onto them for support and staggered over to the mayor, Artie Johnson, a short, bespectacled man. After a brief conversation, Mildred sidled up to him coquettishly, her abundant sausage figure encased in turquoise silk from The Orient. She twirled him around with the grace of a hippo, no doubt stepping on his feet the entire time.

She drew the curtains and sighed deeply. She and Tony were spending their days in exile until all of their affairs were in order and arrangements could be made to move elsewhere. They had furnished the guesthouse sparsely with nothing more than basic necessities for the duration of their stay.

He stirred and opened his eyes.

"Sydney?"

"I'm here, sweetheart." she stroked his hair.

"You've made me happier than I've ever been in my life." he said.

"You've made me happier than I ever imagined possible, Tony."

"Why don't you call Dottie tomorrow morning and tell her you've decided to keep the tentative lunch date you two set up?"

"Are you sure?"

"You deserve a little change of scenery and social interaction with someone other than me."

"This is where I'm most at peace and at my happiest."

"You need a break. Besides, I have a little paperwork to do to wrap things up, so we can leave town."

"In that case…"

"Buy yourself a new dress."

"I want to buy something for you."

"No. Just buy for yourself. I have all I need and want right here." he reached out to her.

"Tony, don't ever let me go." she buried her face in his chest.

"I'll never let you go, Sydney." he kissed her hair, "I'll be by your side, no matter what."

* * *

Dottie cast a solicitous glance at Sydney piercing her cheesecake with her fork as police cars and an ambulance sped down Queen Street toward Waterloo Row.

"Do you want to head back?" she asked her.

Sydney nodded.

Dottie motioned to the waitress to bring the check and the latter complied promptly.

"It's my treat." she told Sydney on her way to the cash register to pay.

Sydney put on her long, lacy white cardigan and followed Dottie outside. They walked briskly in silence for what seemed like endless miles. Sydney froze at the sight of the flashing lights in the Horncastle driveway. Dottie placed an arm around her and called out:

"Excuse me! Can someone please tell us what's going on here?"

"Hi, Dottie." a young officer with a blonde ponytail turned around and smiled, "J.T. is over there. I'll get him for you."

"Thanks, Jill." Dottie patted a trembling Sydney's arm.

"Hi, honey." J.T. was walking toward them.

"What's going on, honey?"

"We just got the call a few minutes ago." he said solemnly, "I'm afraid it's not good, Dots."

"Where's Tony?" Sydney attempted to run to the ambulance. "I want to see Tony."

Then, she froze as the paramedics came out of the mansion with a stretcher. Mildred, Annette, and Donald were behind them. Warren pushed them out of his way to run to Sydney, who collapsed in his arms. Dottie buried her face in J.T.'s chest.

"Tony! I want to see Tony!" Sydney broke free from Warren and ran to the stretcher, "I have to see my Tony!"

"Ma'am, I'm afraid you can't." a middle-aged officer told her.

"Tony..." she attempted to uncover his face, however, was pulled away gently by Jill and Warren.

"You!" Sydney glared accusingly at Mildred, "You! You did this! It's all your fault, you evil woman! You killed my Tony! I'm going to make you pay for this! You'll see. I'm going to destroy your life!"

Mildred let out a dramatic whimper and threw herself into Donald's arms. Annette whispered in her ear. Warren and Jill led the sobbing Sydney away from the ambulance.

"J.T." Warren said, "Can you call Brett? I'm driving Sydney over to her place. I want to be sure she'll be there."

"I'll take care of it." J.T reassured him, motioning to Jill to comfort Dottie.

Warren held Sydney as J.T. ran into the house.

"Tony...Tony..." she was quivering, "I need to see him...I want to be with him."

J.T. returned shortly and nodded at Warren, who attempted to lead Sydney to his car. She disintegrated into a mass of white frothy fabric on the lawn. Without hesitation, he picked her up and carried her. Tony's last words to him were playing over and over in his mind:

"Please take care of Sydney."

* * *

When Brett's doorbell rang, she was in the kitchen, turning off the burner and removing a pot of soup from the stove.

"I'll get it." Sydney said.

"It's probably Mrs. Jones from down the street with that cake recipe."

Sydney opened the door to find a scowling Donald.

"You've got until five o'clock to clear out all your stuff and vacate the premises. Anything left behind is going to be put out on the curb for trash collection and the locks are going to be changed." He glared at her.

Brett appeared behind her with a glare to outdo his.

"Does it make you feel like a big man to terrorize a grieving widow? Ooo, Donald Horncastle, big shot around town! I bet your wife keeps young lovers because you can't get it up! Now, get lost before I have you arrested!"

"Five o'clock." he pointed an index finger at Sydney before turning around.

Before slamming the door, Brett called out:

"I hope your toupee falls in a mud puddle!"

"I guess I'll have to go over there after lunch and get my personal items."

"Don't worry, hon. I've got an idea. I'll call Dottie and ask her to store Tony's things, your household items, and the furniture you two bought in their basement. There's a storage room no one's using. The staff can take it down there and Dottie can arrange to have the lock changed so the rest of the family can't access it. I'll ask her to make one key for you and one for me, as well. Everything should be safe down there. You can bring your personal stuff here."

"Thank you, Brett...You know, they're going to try to keep me from attending his funeral, too. I just know it."

"Don't worry, hon. I have a plan for that, too. You just leave everything to me."

*　*　*

All eyes were averted to the back of the room as the trio entered with linked arms, followed by Leonard, Greeney, and the entire staff of "Dorothy's".

"Hold your head up high, baby." Brett whispered to the unexpectedly upright and determined Sydney, being held up on each side by Brett and Chuck.

"What is that woman doing here?" Mildred shouted, as though on cue. "Get her out of here!"

"I am not going anywhere." Sydney stated coldly, "Tony was my husband, and I have every right to be here."

The trio proceeded to the group of empty seats near the front across the aisle from the Horncastles. Tony's colleagues and friends from the legal profession who were seated in front of them turned around to acknowledge Sydney and whispered condolences. No one noticed the small group taking notes interspersed among the staff members of "Dorothy's".

*　*　*

"The prominent Horncastle family evicts Tony Horncastle's widow the day after his death and attempts to keep her away from his funeral." Brett read aloud, smiling deliciously and held up the newspaper to show Sydney the accompanying photo taken outside following the funeral.

"You look beautiful in this picture, sweetheart. The camera loves you. We won. We exposed them."

"Your plan was ingenious, Brett."

"We stuck it to the almighty Horncastles. They found out they can't push you around. And, I love how Tony stuck it to them, too, the way he funneled the family assets in addition to his own to set up that annuity in your name. You'll have an income from that for the rest of your life."

"I don't deserve it. If he hadn't married me, he'd still be alive. I should have died instead."

"Don't talk like that, sweetheart. Tony loved you very much. He wanted to be sure you'd be taken care of after he was gone. He wanted you to know he did not abandon you."

"He said he'd never leave me. He kept his promise. I feel him with me. Love is eternal. We mortals do, but love never dies."

* * *

Kent filled two glasses with red wine and handed one to a pensive Aydin.

"Still upset about Jack's letter?" he sat beside him.

"He's making a huge mistake."

"I know, but he wants to do the honorable thing."

"Just because he knocked her up, he's going to resign himself to a lifetime of misery in a loveless marriage. He's too damn honorable."

"Maybe he doesn't see it that way, Aydin. Maybe having a kid supersedes all of that."

"He doesn't know his stepmother and that crazy shrink have been apprehended. He doesn't have to hide anymore. He can go home."

"Aydin, please, don't tell me you're going to tell him about this. You know he can't handle it."

"I realize that. My lips are sealed. I just hope he realizes his mistake before it's too late and backs out of this marriage."

"I do, too. I agree with you. He'll live to regret it. That mad scientist Mazot guy is all over the news. They're bound to hear about it in Idaho, too. His true identity is going to be revealed. That could be a game changer for this Ellie girl."

"No doubt. She'll put out even more, to get her hands on his family's money."

"Or freak out when she finds out about the scandal and his brain damage."

"That Mazot guy looks like a character from a horror movie, with his gaunt face, wire-rimmed glasses and bald head."

"Jack's life is a horror movie, Aydin."

"I found out something very interesting today." Aydin smiled mischievously. "When I went down to the mailbox, I ran into Cory, who lives on the ninth floor...you know, the guy who's friendly with Stephen."

"Oh, yes, him. The building gossip monger."

"He told me something I can't get out of my head...Stephen apparently keeps in touch with a couple of guys from that place where he and Jack knew each other...Can't think of the name...Well, Stephen has found out from them that Sydney's new husband is dead...Shot himself in the head..."

"Go away! That can't be true!"

"It's true. Sydney's a widow now."

"Are you planning to tell Jack?"

"I can't decide. I keep going back and forth about it."

"I'm just worried this might cause more heartbreak for Jack. She might not want him back. If he reaches out, only to have his hopes dashed, that could push him over the edge. He might end up like this Tony fellow. We don't know what this Sydney is like."

"According to Jack, she's a saint. But, then, can you trust his Swiss cheese memory?"

"It's best to let sleeping dogs lie. It could stir up a real hornets' nest. Just tell him you're happy for him and let him know we're always here for him anytime he needs friends to talk to."

"You're right. Why don't we watch that movie we taped last night?"

"I'll get the popcorn." Kent rose and went to the kitchen.

* * *

Brett wearily came up the stairs and joined Chuck in the back room. Gene And The Matchmakers were playing "Cavatina", The theme song from "The Deer Hunter".

"She'll be all right." Chuck reassured her and handed her the martini he had ordered for her. "You know it's all for the best. She's got her parents there, her friend Eli, and her aunt and uncle."

"I'll miss her so much."

"She'll miss you, too. But she couldn't possibly stay here; you know that. She made the right decision."

Brett sighed and took a sip of her martini.

"What you need is a good cry. You kept it together for Sydney's sake, but you didn't give yourself a chance to grieve Tony...You two went back a long way."

"I'm so glad he found Sydney. She was the best thing that happened to him. They deserved to have a long life together. But it seems good things never last."

"That's why you've got to hold on to them while you can."

"Summer is a short season." Brett mused, her eyes brimming with tears and raised her martini glass to her lips.

Continued in SUMMER'S ECHO

ABOUT THE AUTHOR:

Summer Seline Coyle has a B.A. in Sociology and English Literature, and a Certificate in Counselling.

Her personal history of extreme abuse, neglect, and injustice is the driving force behind the empathy, tenderness, and passion in her portrayal of her diverse characters. Through her fiction, she hopes to raise public awareness, and be a healing voice for other survivors.

ALSO BY SUMMER SELINE COYLE:

DAISIES FROM ASHES

SCORPIONS HUNT BY NIGHT

SANDCASTLES IN THE RAIN

SUMMER'S ECHO (Formerly SANCTUARY)

Lightning Source UK Ltd.
Milton Keynes UK
UKHW010636220621
385957UK00001B/105